Space Prison
(The Survivors)

Tom Godwin

Space Prison (The Survivors)

Copyright © 2022 Indo-European Publishing

The present edition is a reproduction of previous publication of this classic work. Minor typographical errors may have been corrected without note; however, for an authentic reading experience the spelling, punctuation, and capitalization have been retained from the original text.

ISBN: 978-1-64439-974-3

To

JOE AND BLANCHE KOLARIK, whose friendship and
encouragement in the years gone by will never be forgotten.

PART 1

For seven weeks the Constellation had been plunging through hyperspace with her eight thousand colonists; fleeing like a hunted thing with her communicators silenced and her drives moaning and thundering. Up in the control room, Irene had been told, the needles of the dials danced against the red danger lines day and night.

She lay in bed and listened to the muffled, ceaseless roar of the drives and felt the singing vibration of the hull. We should be almost safe by now, she thought. Athena is only forty days away.

Thinking of the new life awaiting them all made her too restless to lie still any longer. She got up, to sit on the edge of the bed and switch on the light. Dale was gone—he had been summoned to adjust one of the machines in the ship's X-ray room—and Billy was asleep, nothing showing of him above the covers but a crop of brown hair and the furry nose of his ragged teddy bear.

She reached out to straighten the covers, gently, so as not to awaken him. It happened then, the thing they had all feared.

From the stern of the ship came a jarring, deafening explosion. The ship lurched violently, girders screamed, and the light flicked out.

In the darkness she heard a rapid-fire thunk-thunk-thunk as the automatic guard system slid inter-compartment doors shut against sections of the ship suddenly airless. The doors were still thudding shut when another explosion came, from toward the bow. Then there was silence; a feeling of utter quiet and motionlessness.

The fingers of fear enclosed her and her mind said to her, like the cold, unpassionate voice of a stranger: The Gerns have found us.

The light came on again, a feeble glow, and there was the soft, muffled sound of questioning voices in the other compartments. She dressed, her fingers shaking and clumsy, wishing that Dale would come to reassure her; to tell her that nothing really serious had happened, that it had not been the Gerns.

1

It was very still in the little compartment—strangely so. She had finished dressing when she realized the reason: the air circulation system had stopped working.

That meant the power failure was so great that the air regenerators, themselves, were dead. And there were eight thousand people on the Constellation who would have to have air to live....

The Attention buzzer sounded shrilly from the public address system speakers that were scattered down the ship's corridors. A voice she recognized as that of Lieutenant Commander Lake spoke:

"War was declared upon Earth by the Gern Empire ten days ago. Two Gern cruisers have attacked us and their blasters have destroyed the stern and bow of the ship. We are without a drive and without power but for a few emergency batteries. I am the Constellation's only surviving officer and the Gern commander is boarding us to give me the surrender terms.

"None of you will leave your compartments until ordered to do so. Wherever you may be, remain there. This is necessary to avoid confusion and to have as many as possible in known locations for future instructions. I repeat: you will not leave your compartments."

The speaker cut off. She stood without moving and heard again the words: I am the Constellation's only surviving officer....

The Gerns had killed her father.

He had been second-in-command of the Dunbar expedition that had discovered the world of Athena and his knowledge of Athena was valuable to the colonization plans. He had been quartered among the ship's officers—and the Gern blast had destroyed that section of the ship.

She sat down on the edge of the bed again and tried to reorient herself; to accept the fact that her life and the lives of all the others had abruptly, irrevocably, been changed.

The Athena Colonization Plan was ended. They had known such a thing might happen—that was why the Constellation had been made ready for the voyage in secret and had waited for months for the chance to slip through the ring of Gern spy ships; that was why she

2

had raced at full speed, with her communicators silenced so there would be no radiations for the Gerns to find her by. Only forty days more would have brought them to the green and virgin world of Athena, four hundred light-years beyond the outermost boundary of the Gern Empire. There they should have been safe from Gern detection for many years to come; for long enough to build planetary defenses against attack. And there they would have used Athena's rich resources to make ships and weapons to defend mineral-depleted Earth against the inexorably increasing inclosure of the mighty, coldly calculating colossus that was the Gern Empire.

Success or failure of the Athena Plan had meant ultimate life or death for Earth. They had taken every precaution possible but the Gern spy system had somehow learned of Athena and the Constellation. Now, the cold war was no longer cold and the Plan was dust....

Billy sighed and stirred in the little-boy sleep that had not been broken by the blasts that had altered the lives of eight thousand people and the fate of a world.

She shook his shoulder and said, "Billy."

He raised up, so small and young to her eyes that the question in her mind was like an anguished prayer: Dear God—what do Gerns do to five-year-old boys?

He saw her face, and the dim light, and the sleepiness was suddenly gone from him. "What's wrong, Mama? And why are you scared?"

There was no reason to lie to him.

"The Gerns found us and stopped us."

"Oh," he said. In his manner was the grave thoughtfulness of a boy twice his age, as there always was. "Will they—will they kill us?"

"Get dressed, honey," she said. "Hurry, so we'll be ready when they let Daddy come back to tell us what to do."

They were both ready when the Attention buzzer sounded again in the corridors. Lake spoke, his tone grim and bitter:

3

"There is no power for the air regenerators and within twenty hours we will start smothering to death. Under these circumstances I could not do other than accept the survival terms the Gern commander offered us.

"He will speak to you now and you will obey his orders without protest. Death is the only alternative."

Then the voice of the Gern commander came, quick and harsh and brittle:

"This section of space, together with planet Athena, is an extension of the Gern Empire. This ship has deliberately invaded Gern territory in time of war with intent to seize and exploit a Gern world. We are willing, however, to offer a leniency not required by the circumstances. Terran technicians and skilled workers in certain fields can be used in the factories we shall build on Athena. The others will not be needed and there is not room on the cruisers to take them.

"Your occupation records will be used to divide you into two groups: the Acceptables and the Rejects. The Rejects will be taken by the cruisers to an Earth-type planet near here and left, together with the personal possessions in their compartments and additional, and ample, supplies. The Acceptables will then be taken on to Athena and at a later date the cruisers will return the Rejects to Earth.

"This division will split families but there will be no resistance to it. Gern guards will be sent immediately to make this division and you will wait in your compartments for them. You will obey their orders promptly and without annoying them with questions. At the first instance of resistance or rebellion this offer will be withdrawn and the cruisers will go their way again."

In the silence following the ultimatum she could hear the soft, wordless murmur from the other compartments, the undertone of anxiety like a dark thread through it. In every compartment parents and children, brothers and sisters, were seeing one another for the last time....

The corridor outside rang to the tramp of feet; the sound of a dozen Gerns walking with swift military precision. She held her breath, her

4

heart racing, but they went past her door and on to the corridor's end.

There she could faintly hear them entering compartments, demanding names, and saying, "Out—out!" Once she heard a Gern say, "Acceptables will remain inside until further notice. Do not open your doors after the Rejects have been taken out."

Billy touched her on the hand. "Isn't Daddy going to come?"

"He—he can't right now. We'll see him pretty soon."

She remembered what the Gern commander had said about the Rejects being permitted to take their personal possessions. She had very little time in which to get together what she could carry....

There were two small bags in the compartment and she hurried to pack them with things she and Dale and Billy might need, not able to know which of them, if any, would be Rejects. Nor could she know whether she should put in clothes for a cold world or a hot one. The Gern commander had said the Rejects would be left on an Earth-type planet but where could it be? The Dunbar Expedition had explored across five hundred light-years of space and had found only one Earth-type world: Athena.

The Gerns were almost to her door when she had finished and she heard them enter the compartments across from her own. There came the hard, curt questions and the command: "Outside—hurry!" A woman said something in pleading question and there was the soft thud of a blow and the words: "Outside—do not ask questions!" A moment later she heard the woman going down the corridor, trying to hold back her crying.

Then the Gerns were at her own door.

She held Billy's hand and waited for them with her heart hammering. She held her head high and composed herself with all the determination she could muster so that the arrogant Gerns would not see that she was afraid. Billy stood beside her as tall as his five years would permit, his teddy bear under his arm, and only the way his hand held to hers showed that he, too, was scared.

The door was flung open and two Gerns strode in.

5

The were big, dark men, with powerful, bulging muscles. They surveyed her and the room with a quick sweep of eyes that were like glittering obsidian, their mouths thin, cruel slashes in the flat, brutal planes of their faces.

"Your name?" snapped the one who carried a sheaf of occupation records.

"It's"—she tried to swallow the quaver in her voice and make it cool and unfrightened—"Irene Lois Humbolt—Mrs. Dale Humbolt."

The Gern glanced at the papers. "Where is your husband?"

"He was in the X-ray room at—"

"You are a Reject. Out—down the corridor with the others."

"My husband—will he be a—"

"Outside!"

It was the tone of voice that had preceded the blow in the other compartment and the Gern took a quick step toward her. She seized the two bags in one hand, not wanting to release Billy, and swung back to hurry out into the corridor. The other Gern jerked one of the bags from her hand and flung it to the floor. "Only one bag per person," he said, and gave her an impatient shove that sent her and Billy stumbling through the doorway.

She became part of the Rejects who were being herded like sheep down the corridors and into the port airlock. There were many children among them, the young ones frightened and crying, and often with only one parent or an older brother or sister to take care of them. And there were many young ones who had no one at all and were dependent upon strangers to take their hands and tell them what they must do.

When she was passing the corridor that led to the X-ray room she saw a group of Rejects being herded up it. Dale was not among them and she knew, then, that she and Billy would never see him again.

"Out from the ship—faster—faster——"

6

The commands of the Gern guards snapped like whips around them as she and the other Rejects crowded and stumbled down the boarding ramp and out onto the rocky ground. There was the pull of a terrible gravity such as she had never experienced and they were in a bleak, barren valley, a cold wind moaning down it and whipping the alkali dust in bitter clouds. Around the valley stood ragged hills, their white tops laying out streamers of wind-driven snow, and the sky was dark with sunset.

"Out from the ship—faster——"

It was hard to walk fast in the high gravity, carrying the bag in one hand and holding up all of Billy's weight she could with the other.

"They lied to us!" a man beside her said to someone. "Let's turn and fight. Let's take——"

A Gern blaster cracked with a vivid blue flash and the man plunged lifelessly to the ground. She flinched instinctively and fell over an unseen rock, the bag of precious clothes flying from her hand. She scrambled up again, her left knee half numb, and turned to retrieve it.

The Gern guard was already upon her, his blaster still in his hand. "Out from the ship—faster."

The barrel of his blaster lashed across the side of her head. "Move on—move on!"

She staggered in a blinding blaze of pain and then hurried on, holding tight to Billy's hand, the wind cutting like knives of ice through her thin clothes and blood running in a trickle down her cheek.

"He hit you," Billy said. "He hurt you." Then he called the Gern a name that five-year-old boys were not supposed to know, with a savagery that five-year-old boys were not supposed to possess.

When she stopped at the outer fringe of Rejects she saw that all of them were out of the cruiser and the guards were going back into it. A half mile down the valley the other cruiser stood, the Rejects out from it and its boarding ramps already withdrawn.

When she had buttoned Billy's blouse tighter and wiped the blood

7

from her face the first blast of the drives came from the farther cruiser. The nearer one blasted a moment later and they lifted together, their roaring filling the valley. They climbed faster and faster, dwindling as they went. Then they disappeared in the black sky, their roaring faded away, and there was left only the moaning of the wind around her and somewhere a child crying.

And somewhere a voice asking, "Where are we? In the name of God—what have they done to us?"

She looked at the snow streaming from the ragged hills, felt the hard pull of the gravity, and knew where they were. They were on Ragnarok, the hell-world of 1.5 gravity and fierce beasts and raging fevers where men could not survive. The name came from an old Teutonic myth and meant: The last day for gods and men. The Dunbar Expedition had discovered Ragnarok and her father had told her of it, of how it had killed six of the eight men who had left the ship and would have killed all of them if they had remained any longer.

She knew where they were and she knew the Gerns had lied to them and would never send a ship to take them to Earth. Their abandonment there had been intended as a death sentence for all of them.

And Dale was gone and she and Billy would die helpless and alone....

"It will be dark—so soon." Billy's voice shook with the cold. "If Daddy can't find us in the dark, what will we do?"

"I don't know," she said. "There's no one to help us and how can I know—what we should do——"

She was from the city. How could she know what to do on an alien, hostile world where armed explorers had died? She had tried to be brave before the Gerns but now—now night was at hand and out of it would come terror and death for herself and Billy. They would never see Dale again, never see Athena or Earth or even the dawn on the world that had killed them....

She tried not to cry, and failed. Billy's cold little hand touched her own, trying to reassure her.

8

"Don't cry, Mama. I guess—I guess everybody else is scared, too."

Everyone else....

She was not alone. How could she have thought she was alone? All around her were others, as helpless and uncertain as she. Her story was only one out of four thousand.

"I guess they are, Billy," she said. "I never thought of that, before."

She knelt to put her arms around him, thinking: Tears and fear are futile weapons; they can never bring us any tomorrows. We'll have to fight whatever comes to kill us no matter how scared we are. For ourselves and for our children. Above all else, for our children....

"I'm going back to find our clothes," she said. "You wait here for me, in the shelter of that rock, and I won't be gone long."

Then she told him what he would be too young to really understand.

"I'm not going to cry any more and I know, now, what I must do. I'm going to make sure that there is a tomorrow for you, always, to the last breath of my life."

The bright blue star dimmed and the others faded away. Dawn touched the sky, bringing with it a coldness that frosted the steel of the rifle in John Prentiss's hands and formed beads of ice on his gray mustache. There was a stirring in the area behind him as the weary Rejects prepared to face the new day and the sound of a child whimpering from the cold. There had been no time the evening before to gather wood for fires——

"Prowlers!"

The warning cry came from an outer guard and black shadows were suddenly sweeping out of the dark dawn.

They were things that might have been half wolf, half tiger; each of them three hundred pounds of incredible ferocity with eyes blazing like yellow fire in their white-fanged tiger-wolf faces. They came like the wind, in a flowing black wave, and ripped through the outer guard line as though it had not existed. The inner guards fired in a

9

chattering roll of gunshots, trying to turn them, and Prentiss's rifle licked out pale tongues of flame as he added his own fire. The prowlers came on, breaking through, but part of them went down and the others were swerved by the fire so that they struck only the outer edge of the area where the Rejects were grouped.

At that distance they blended into the dark ground so that he could not find them in the sights of his rifle. He could only watch helplessly and see a dark-haired woman caught in their path, trying to run with a child in her arms and already knowing it was too late. A man was running toward her, slow in the high gravity, an axe in his hands and his cursing a raging, savage snarl. For a moment her white face was turned in helpless appeal to him and the others; then the prowlers were upon her and she fell, deliberately, going to the ground with her child hugged in her arms beneath her so that her body would protect it.

The prowlers passed over her, pausing for an instant to slash the life from her, and raced on again. They vanished back into the outer darkness, the farther guards firing futilely, and there was a silence but for the distant, hysterical sobbing of a woman.

It had happened within seconds; the fifth prowler attack that night and the mildest.

Full dawn had come by the time he replaced the guards killed by the last attack and made the rounds of the other guard lines. He came back by the place where the prowlers had killed the woman, walking wearily against the pull of gravity. She lay with her dark hair tumbled and stained with blood, her white face turned up to the reddening sky, and he saw her clearly for the first time.

It was Irene.

He stopped, gripping the cold steel of the rifle and not feeling the rear sight as it cut into his hand.

Irene.... He had not known she was on Ragnarok. He had not seen her in the darkness of the night and he had hoped she and Billy were safe among the Acceptables with Dale.

There was the sound of footsteps and a bold-faced girl in a red skirt stopped beside him, her glance going over him curiously.

10

"The little boy," he asked, "do you know if he's all right?"

"The prowlers cut up his face but he'll be all right," she said. "I came back after his clothes."

"Are you going to look after him?"

"Someone has to and"—she shrugged her shoulders—"I guess I was soft enough to elect myself for the job. Why—was his mother a friend of yours?"

"She was my daughter," he said.

"Oh." For a moment the bold, brassy look was gone from her face, like a mask that had slipped. "I'm sorry. And I'll take care of Billy."

The first objection to his assumption of leadership occurred an hour later. The prowlers had withdrawn with the coming of full daylight and wood had been carried from the trees to build fires. Mary, one of the volunteer cooks, was asking two men to carry her some water when he approached. The smaller man picked up one of the clumsy containers, hastily improvised from canvas, and started toward the creek. The other, a big, thick-chested man, did not move.

"We'll have to have water," Mary said. "People are hungry and cold and sick."

The man continued to squat by the fire, his hands extended to its warmth. "Name someone else," he said.

"But——"

She looked at Prentiss in uncertainty. He went to the thick-chested man, knowing there would be violence and welcoming it as something to help drive away the vision of Irene's pale, cold face under the red sky.

"She asked you to get her some water," he said. "Get it."

The man looked up at him, studying him with deliberate insolence, then he got to his feet, his heavy shoulders hunched challengingly.

"I'll have to set you straight, old timer," he said. "No one has

11

appointed you the head cheese around here. Now, there's the container you want filled and over there"—he made a small motion with one hand—"is the creek. Do you know what to do?"

"Yes," he said. "I know what to do."

He brought the butt of the rifle smashing up. It struck the man under the chin and there was a sharp cracking sound as his jawbone snapped. For a fraction of a second there was an expression of stupefied amazement on his face then his eyes glazed and he slumped to the ground with his broken jaw setting askew.

"All right," he said to Mary. "Now you go ahead and name somebody else."

He found that the prowlers had killed seventy during the night. One hundred more had died from the Hell Fever that often followed exposure and killed within an hour.

He went the half mile to the group that had arrived on the second cruiser as soon as he had eaten a delayed breakfast. He saw, before he had quite reached the other group, that the Constellation's Lieutenant Commander, Vincent Lake, was in charge of it.

Lake, a tall, hard-jawed man with pale blue eyes under pale brows, walked forth to meet him as soon as he recognized him.

"Glad to see you're still alive," Lake greeted him. "I thought that second Gern blast got you along with the others."

"I was visiting midship and wasn't home when it happened," he said.

He looked at Lake's group of Rejects, in their misery and uncertainty so much like his own, and asked, "How was it last night?"

"Bad—damned bad," Lake said. "Prowlers and Hell Fever, and no wood for fires. Two hundred died last night."

"I came down to see if anyone was in charge here and to tell them that we'll have to move into the woods at once—today. We'll have

12

plenty of wood for the fires there, some protection from the wind, and by combining our defenses we can stand off the prowlers better."

Lake agreed. When the brief discussion of plans was finished he asked, "How much do you know about Ragnarok?"

"Not much," Prentiss answered. "We didn't stay to study it very long. There are no heavy metals on Ragnarok's other sun. Its position in the advance of the resources of any value. We gave Ragnarok a quick survey and when the sixth man died we marked it on the chart as uninhabitable and went on our way.

"As you probably know, that bright blue star is Ragnarok's other sun. It's position in the advance of the yellow sun shows the season to be early spring. When summer comes Ragnarok will swing between the two suns and the heat will be something no human has ever endured. Nor the cold, when winter comes.

"I know of no edible plants, although there might be some. There are a few species of rodent-like animals—they're scavengers—and a herbivore we called the woods goat. The prowlers are the dominant form of life on Ragnarok and I suspect their intelligence is a good deal higher than we would like it to be. There will be a constant battle for survival with them.

"There's another animal, not as intelligent as the prowlers but just as dangerous—the unicorn. The unicorns are big and fast and they travel in herds. I haven't seen any here so far—I hope we don't. At the lower elevations are the swamp crawlers. They're unadulterated nightmares. I hope they don't go to these higher elevations in the summer. The prowlers and the Hell Fever, the gravity and heat and cold and starvation, will be enough for us to have to fight."

"I see," Lake said. He smiled, a smile that was as bleak as moonlight on an arctic glacier. "Earth-type—remember the promise the Gerns made the Rejects?" He looked out across the camp, at the snow whipping from the frosty hills, at the dead and the dying, and a little girl trying vainly to awaken her brother.

"They were condemned, without reason, without a chance to live," he said. "So many of them are so young ... and when you're young it's too soon to have to die."

13

Prentiss returned to his own group. The dead were buried in shallow graves and inventory was taken of the promised "ample supplies." These were only the few personal possessions the Rejects had been permitted to take plus a small amount of food the Gerns had taken from the Constellation's stores. The Gerns had been forced to provide the Rejects with at least a little food—had they openly left them to starve, the Acceptables, whose families were among the Rejects, might have rebelled.

Inventory of the firearms and ammunition showed the total to be discouragingly small. They would have to learn how to make and use bows and arrows as soon as possible.

With the first party of guards and workmen following him, Prentiss went to the tributary valley that emptied into the central valley a mile to the north. It was as good a camp site as could be hoped for; wide and thickly spotted with groves of trees, a creek running down its center.

The workmen began the construction of shelters and he climbed up the side of the nearer hill. He reached its top, his breath coming fast in the gravity that was the equivalent of a burden half his own weight, and saw what the surrounding terrain was like.

To the south, beyond the barren valley, the land could be seen dropping in its long sweep to the southern lowlands where the unicorns and swamp crawlers lived. To the north the hills climbed gently for miles, then ended under the steeply sloping face of an immense plateau. The plateau reached from western to eastern horizon, still white with the snows of winter and looming so high above the world below that the clouds brushed it and half obscured it.

He went back down the hill as Lake's men appeared. They started work on what would be a continuation of his own camp and he told Lake what he had seen from the hill.

"We're between the lowlands and the highlands," he said. "This will be as near to a temperate altitude as Ragnarok has. We survive here—or else. There's no other place for us to go."

An overcast darkened the sky at noon and the wind died down to almost nothing. There was a feeling of waiting tension in the air and he went back to the Rejects, to speed their move into the woods. They were already going in scattered groups, accompanied by prowler guards, but there was no organization and it would be too long before the last of them were safely in the new camp.

He could not be two places at once—he needed a subleader to oversee the move of the Rejects and their possessions into the woods and their placement after they got there.

He found the man he wanted already helping the Rejects get started: a thin, quiet man named Henry Anders who had fought well against the prowlers the night before, even though his determination had been greater than his marksmanship. He was the type people instinctively liked and trusted; a good choice for the subleader whose job it would be to handle the multitude of details in camp while he, Prentiss, and a second subleader he would select, handled the defense of the camp and the hunting.

"I don't like this overcast," he told Anders. "Something's brewing. Get everyone moved and at work helping build shelters as soon as you can."

"I can have most of them there within an hour or two," Anders said. "Some of the older people, though, will have to take it slow. This gravity—it's already getting the hearts of some of them."

"How are the children taking the gravity?" he asked.

"The babies and the very young—it's hard to tell about them yet. But the children from about four on up get tired quickly, go to sleep, and when they wake up they've sort of bounced back out of it."

"Maybe they can adapt to some extent to this gravity." He thought of what Lake had said that morning: So many of them are so young ... and when you're young it's too soon to have to die. "Maybe the Gerns made a mistake—maybe Terran children aren't as easy to kill as they thought. It's your job and mine and others to give the children the chance to prove the Gerns wrong."

He went his way again to pass by the place where Julia, the girl who had become Billy's foster-mother, was preparing to go to the new camp.

15

It was the second time for him to see Billy that morning. The first time Billy had still been stunned with grief, and at the sight of his grandfather he had been unable to keep from breaking.

"The Gern hit her," he had sobbed, his torn face bleeding anew as it twisted in crying. "He hurt her, and Daddy was gone and then—and then the other things killed her——"

But now he had had a little time to accept what had happened and he was changed. He was someone much older, almost a man, trapped for a while in the body of a five-year-old boy.

"I guess this is all, Billy," Julia was saying as she gathered up her scanty possessions and Irene's bag. "Get your teddy bear and we'll go."

Billy went to his teddy bear and knelt down to pick it up. Then he stopped and said something that sounded like "No." He laid the teddy bear back down, wiping a little dust from its face as in a last gesture of farewell, and stood up to face Julia empty-handed.

"I don't think I'll want to play with my teddy bear any more," he said. "I don't think I'll ever want to play at all anymore."

Then he went to walk beside her, leaving his teddy bear lying on the ground behind him and with it leaving forever the tears and laughter of childhood.

The overcast deepened, and at midafternoon dark storm clouds came driving in from the west. Efforts were intensified to complete the move before the storm broke, both in his section of the camp and in Lake's. The shelters would be of critical importance and they were being built of the materials most quickly available; dead limbs, brush, and the limited amount of canvas and blankets the Rejects had. They would be inadequate protection but there was no time to build anything better.

It seemed only a few minutes until the black clouds were overhead, rolling and racing at an incredible velocity. With them came the deep roar of the high wind that drove them and the wind on the ground began to stir restlessly in response, like some monster awakening to the call of its kind.

Prentiss knew already who he wanted as his other subleader. He found him hard at work helping build shelters; Howard Craig, a powerfully muscled man with a face as hard and grim as a cliff of granite. It had been Craig who had tried to save Irene from the prowlers that morning with only an axe as a weapon.

Prentiss knew him slightly—and Craig still did not know Irene had been his daughter. Craig had been one of the field engineers for what would have been the Athena Geological Survey. He had had a wife, a frail, blonde girl who had been the first of all to die of Hell Fever the night before, and he still had their three small children.

"We'll stop with the shelters we already have built," he told Craig. "It will take all the time left to us to reinforce them against the wind. I need someone to help me, in addition to Anders. You're the one I want.

"Send some young and fast-moving men back to last night's camp to cut all the strips of prowler skins they can get. Everything about the shelters will have to be lashed down to something solid. See if you can find some experienced outdoorsmen to help you check the jobs.

"And tell Anders that women and children only will be placed in the shelters. There will be no room for anyone else and if any man, no matter what the excuse, crowds out a woman or child I'll personally kill him."

"You needn't bother," Craig said. He smiled with savage mirthlessness. "I'll be glad to take care of any such incidents."

Prentiss saw to it that the piles of wood for the guard fires were ready to be lighted when the time came. He ordered all guards to their stations, there to get what rest they could. They would have no rest at all after darkness came.

He met Lake at the north end of his own group's camp, where it merged with Lake's group and no guard line was needed. Lake told him that his camp would be as well prepared as possible under the circumstances within another hour. By then the wind in the trees was growing swiftly stronger, slapping harder and harder at the shelters, and it seemed doubtful that the storm would hold off for an hour.

But Lake was given his hour, plus half of another. Then deep dusk

17

came, although it was not quite sundown. Prentiss ordered all the guard fires lighted and all the women and children into the shelters. Fifteen minutes later the storm finally broke.

It came as a roaring downpour of cold rain. Complete darkness came with it and the wind rose to a velocity that made the trees lean. An hour went by and the wind increased, smashing at the shelters with a violence they had not been built to withstand. The prowler skin lashings held but the canvas and blankets were ripped into streamers that cracked like rifle shots in the wind before they were torn completely loose and flung into the night.

One by one the guard fires went out and the rain continued, growing colder and driven in almost horizontal sheets by the wind. The women and children huddled in chilled misery in what meager protection the torn shelters still gave and there was nothing that could be done to help them.

The rain turned to snow at midnight, a howling blizzard through which Prentiss's light could penetrate but a few feet as he made his rounds. He walked with slogging weariness, forcing himself on. He was no longer young—he was fifty—and he had had little rest.

He had known, of course, that successful leadership would involve more sacrifice on his part than on the part of those he led. He could have shunned responsibility and his personal welfare would have benefited. He had lived on alien worlds almost half his life; with a rifle and a knife he could have lived, until Ragnarok finally killed him, with much less effort than that required of him as leader. But such an action had been repugnant to him, unthinkable. What he knew of survival on hostile worlds might help the others to survive.

So he had assumed command, tolerating no objections and disregarding the fact that he would be shortening his already short time to live on Ragnarok. It was, he supposed, some old instinct that forbade the individual to stand aside and let the group die.

The snow stopped an hour later and the wind died to a frigid moaning. The clouds thinned, broke apart, and the giant star looked down upon the land with its cold, blue light.

The prowlers came then.

They feinted against the east and west guard lines, then hit the south line in massed, ferocious attack. Twenty got through, past the slaughtered south guards, and charged into the interior of the camp. As they did so the call, prearranged by him in case of such an event, went up the guard lines:

"Emergency guards, east and west—close in!"

In the camp, above the triumphant, demoniac yammering of the prowlers, came the screams of women, the thinner cries of children, and the shouting and cursing of men as they tried to fight the prowlers with knives and clubs. Then the emergency guards—every third man from the east and west lines—came plunging through the snow, firing as they came.

The prowlers launched themselves away from their victims and toward the guards, leaving a woman to stagger aimlessly with blood spurting from a severed artery and splashing dark in the starlight on the blue-white snow. The air was filled with the cracking of gunfire and the deep, savage snarling of the prowlers. Half of the prowlers broke through, leaving seven dead guards behind them. The others lay in the snow where they had fallen and the surviving emergency guards turned to hurry back to their stations, reloading as they went.

The wounded woman had crumpled down in the snow and a first aid man knelt over her. He straightened, shaking his head, and joined the others as they searched for injured among the prowlers' victims.

They found no injured; only the dead. The prowlers killed with grim efficiency.

"John——"

John Chiara, the young doctor, hurried toward him. His dark eyes were worried behind his frosted glasses and his eyebrows were coated with ice.

"The wood is soaked," he said. "It's going to be some time before we can get fires going. There are babies that will freeze to death before then."

Prentiss looked at the prowlers lying in the snow and motioned toward them. "They're warm. Have their guts and lungs taken out."

19

"What——"

Then Chiara's eyes lighted with comprehension and he hurried away without further questions.

Prentiss went on, to make the rounds of the guards. When he returned he saw that his order had been obeyed.

The prowlers lay in the snow as before, their savage faces still twisted in their dying snarls, but snug and warm inside them babies slept.

The prowlers attacked again and again and when the wan sun lifted to shine down on the white, frozen land there were five hundred dead in Prentiss's camp: three hundred by Hell Fever and two hundred by prowler attacks.

Five hundred—and that had been only one night on Ragnarok.

Lake reported over six hundred dead. "I hope," he said with bitter hatred, "that the Gerns slept comfortably last night."

"We'll have to build a wall around the camp to hold out the prowlers," Prentiss said. "We don't dare keep using up what little ammunition we have at the rate we've used it the last two nights."

"That will be a big job in this gravity," Lake said. "We'll have to crowd both groups in together to let its circumference be as small as possible."

It was the way Prentiss had planned to do it. One thing would have to be settled with Lake: there could not be two independent leaders over the merged groups.

Lake, watching him, said, "I think we can get along. Alien worlds are your specialty rather than mine. And according to the Ragnarok law of averages, there will be only one of us pretty soon, anyway."

All were moved to the center of the camp area that day and when the prowlers came that night they found a ring of guards and fires through which they could penetrate only with heavy sacrifices.

There was warmth to the sun the next morning and the snow began to melt. Work was commenced on the stockade wall. It would have to be twelve feet high so the prowlers could not jump over it and, since the prowlers had the sharp claws and climbing ability of cats, its top would have to be surmounted with a row of sharp outward-and-downward projecting stakes. These would be set in sockets in the top rail and tied down with strips of prowler skin.

The trees east of camp were festooned for a great distance with the remnants of canvas and cloth the wind had left there. A party of boys, protected by the usual prowler guards, was sent out to climb the trees and recover it. All of it, down to the smallest fragment, was turned over to the women who were physically incapable of helping work on the stockade wall. They began patiently sewing the rags and tatters back into usable form again.

The first hunting party went out and returned with six of the tawny-yellow sharp-horned woods goats, each as large as an Earth deer. The hunters reported the woods goats to be hard to stalk and dangerous when cornered. One hunter was killed and another injured because of not knowing that.

They also brought in a few of the rabbit-sized scavenger animals. They were all legs and teeth and bristly fur, the meat almost inedible. It would be a waste of the limited ammunition to shoot any more of them.

There was a black barked tree which the Dunbar Expedition had called the lance tree because of its slender, straightly outthrust limbs. Its wood was as hard as hickory and as springy as cedar. Prentiss found two amateur archers who were sure they could make efficient bows and arrows out of the lance tree limbs. He gave them the job, together with helpers.

The days turned suddenly hot, with nights that still went below freezing. The Hell Fever took a constant, relentless toll. They needed adequate shelters—but the dwindling supply of ammunition and the nightly prowler attacks made the need for a stockade wall even more imperative. The shelters would have to wait.

He went looking for Dr. Chiara one evening and found him just leaving one of the makeshift shelters.

A boy lay inside it, his face flushed with Hell Fever and his eyes too

21

bright and too dark as he looked up into the face of his mother who sat beside him. She was dry-eyed and silent as she looked down at him but she was holding his hand in hers, tightly, desperately, as though she might that way somehow keep him from leaving her.

Prentiss walked beside Chiara and when the shelter was behind them he asked, "There's no hope?"

"None," Chiara said. "There never is with Hell Fever."

Chiara had changed. He was no longer the stocky, cheerful man he had been on the Constellation, whose brown eyes had smiled at the world through thick glasses and who had laughed and joked as he assured his patients that all would soon be well with them. He was thin and his face was haggard with worry. He had, in his quiet way, been fully as valiant as any of those who had fought the prowlers. He had worked day and night to fight a form of death he could not see and against which he had no weapon.

"The boy is dying," Chiara said. "He knows it and his mother knows it. I told them the medicine I gave him might help. It was a lie, to try to make it a little easier for both of them before the end comes. The medicine I gave him was a salt tablet—that's all I have."

And then, with the first bitterness Prentiss had ever seen him display, Chiara said, "You call me 'Doctor.' Everyone does. I'm not—I'm only a first-year intern. I do the best I know how to do but it isn't enough—it will never be enough."

"What you have to learn here is something no Earth doctor knows or could teach you," he said. "You have to have time to learn—and you need equipment and drugs."

"If I could have antibiotics and other drugs ... I wanted to get a supply from the dispensary but the Gerns wouldn't let me go."

"Some of the Ragnarok plants might be of value if a person could find the right ones. I just came from a talk with Anders about that. He'll provide you with anything possible in the way of equipment and supplies for research—anything in the camp you need to try to save lives. He'll be at your shelter tonight to see what you want. Do you want to try it?"

"Yes—of course." Chiara's eyes lighted with new hope. "It might take a long time to find a cure—maybe we never would—but I'd like to have help so I could try. I'd like to be able, some day once again, to say to a scared kid, 'Take this medicine and in the morning you'll be better,' and know I told the truth."

The nightly prowler attacks continued and the supply of ammunition diminished. It would be some time before men were skilled in the use of the bows and arrows that were being made; and work on the wall was pushed ahead with all speed possible. No one was exempt from labor on it who could as much as carry the pointed stakes. Children down to the youngest worked alongside the men and women.

The work was made many times more exhausting by the 1.5 gravity. People moved heavily at their jobs and even at night there was no surcease from the gravity. They could only go into a coma-like sleep in which there was no real rest and from which they awoke tired and aching. Each morning there would be some who did not awaken at all, though their hearts had been sound enough for working on Earth or Athena.

The killing labor was recognized as necessary, however, and there were no complaints until the morning he was accosted by Peter Bemmon.

He had seen Bemmon several times on the Constellation; a big, soft-faced man who had attached much importance to his role as a minor member of the Athena Planning Board. But even on the Constellation Bemmon had felt he merited a still higher position, and his ingratiating attitude when before his superiors had become one of fault-finding insinuations concerning their ability as compared with his when their backs were turned.

This resentment had taken new form on Ragnarok, where his former position was of utterly no importance to anyone and his lack of any skills or outdoor experience made him only one worker among others.

The sun was shining mercilessly hot the day Bemmon chose to challenge Prentiss's wisdom as leader. Bemmon was cutting and sharpening stakes, a job the sometimes-too-lenient Anders had given him when Bemmon had insisted his heart was on the verge of failure from doing heavier work. Prentiss was in a hurry and would have gone on past him but Bemmon halted him with a sharp command:

"You—wait a minute!"

Bemmon had a hatchet in his hand, but only one stake lay on the ground; and his face was red with anger, not exertion. Prentiss stopped, wondering if Bemmon was going to ask for a broken jaw, and Bemmon came to him.

"How long," Bemmon asked, anger making his voice a little thick, "do you think I'll tolerate this absurd situation?"

"What situation?" Prentiss asked.

"This stupid insistence upon confining me to manual labor. I'm the single member on Ragnarok of the Athena Planning Board and surely you can see that this bumbling confusion of these people"— Bemmon indicated the hurrying, laboring men, women and children around them—"can be transformed into efficient, organized effort only through proper supervision. Yet my abilities along such lines are ignored and I've been forced to work as a common laborer—a wood chopper!"

He flung the hatchet down viciously, into the rocks at his feet, breathing heavily with resentment and challenge. "I demand the respect to which I'm entitled."

"Look," Prentiss said.

He pointed to the group just then going past them. A sixteen-year-old girl was bent almost double under the weight of the pole she was carrying, her once pretty face flushed and sweating. Behind her two twelve-year-old boys were dragging a still larger pole. Behind them came several small children, each of them carrying as many of the pointed stakes as he or she could walk under, no matter if it was only one. All of them were trying to hurry, to accomplish as much as possible, and no one was complaining even though they were already staggering with weariness.

"So you think you're entitled to more respect?" Prentiss asked. "Those kids would work harder if you were giving them orders from under the shade of a tree—is that what you want?"

24

Bemmon's lips thinned and hatred was like a sheen on his face. Prentiss looked from the single stake Bemmon had cut that morning to Bemmon's white, unblistered hands. He looked at the hatchet that Bemmon had thrown down in the rocks and at the V notch broken in its keen-edged blade. It had been the best of the very few hatchets they had....

"The next time you even nick that hatchet I'm going to split your skull with it," he said. "Pick it up and get back to work. I mean work. You'll have broken blisters on every finger tonight or you'll go on the log-carrying force tomorrow. Now, move!"

What Bemmon had thought to be his wrath deserted him before Prentiss's fury. He stooped to obey the order but the hatred remained on his face and when the hatchet was in his hands he made a last attempt to bluster:

"The day may come when we'll refuse to tolerate any longer your sadistic displays of authority."

"Good," Prentiss said. "Anyone who doesn't like my style is welcome to try to change it—or to try to replace me. With knives or clubs, rifles or broken hatchets, Bemmon—any way you want it and any time you want it."

"I——" Bemmon's eyes went from the hatchet in his half raised hand to the long knife in Prentiss's belt. He swallowed with a convulsive jerk of his Adam's apple and his hatchet-bearing arm suddenly wilted. "I don't want to fight—to replace you——"

He swallowed again and his face forced itself into a sickly attempt at an ingratiating smile. "I didn't mean to imply any disrespect for you or the good job you're doing. I'm very sorry."

Then he hurried away, like a man glad to escape, and began to chop stakes with amazing speed.

But the sullen hatred had not been concealed by the ingratiating smile; and Prentiss knew Bemmon was a man who would always be his enemy.

The days dragged by in the weary routine, but overworked muscles

25

slowly strengthened and people moved with a little less laborious effort. On the twentieth day the wall was finally completed and the camp was prowler proof.

But the spring weather was a mad succession of heat and cold and storm that caused the Hell Fever to take its toll each day and there was no relaxation from the grueling labor. Weatherproof shelters had to be built as rapidly as possible.

So the work of constructing them began; wearily, sometimes almost hopelessly, but without complaint other than to hate and curse the Gerns more than ever.

There was no more trouble from Bemmon; Prentiss had almost forgotten him when he was publicly challenged one night by a burly, threatening man named Haggar.

"You've bragged that you'll fight any man who dares disagree with you," Haggar said loudly. "Well, here I am. We'll use knives and before they even have time to bury you tonight I'm goin' to have your stooges kicked out and replaced with men who'll give us competent leadership instead of blunderin' authoritarianism."

Prentiss noticed that Haggar seemed to have a little difficulty pronouncing the last word, as though he had learned it only recently.

"I'll be glad to accommodate you," Prentiss said mildly. "Go get yourself a knife."

Haggar already had one, a long-bladed butcher knife, and the duel began. Haggar was surprisingly adept with his knife but he had never had the training and experience in combat that interstellar explorers such as Prentiss had. Haggar was good, but considerably far from good enough.

Prentiss did not kill him. He had no compunctions about doing such a thing, but it would have been an unnecessary waste of needed manpower. He gave Haggar a carefully painful and bloody lesson that thoroughly banished all his lust for conflict without seriously injuring him. The duel was over within a minute after it began.

Bemmon, who had witnessed the challenge with keen interest and

26

then watched Haggar's defeat with agitation, became excessively friendly and flattering toward Prentiss afterward. Prentiss felt sure, although he had no proof, that it had been Bemmon who had spurred the simple-minded Haggar into challenging him to a duel.

If so, the sight of what had happened to Haggar must have effectively dampened Bemmon's desire for revenge because he became almost a model worker.

As Lake had predicted, he and Prentiss worked together well. Lake calmly took a secondary role, not at all interested in possession of authority but only in the survival of the Rejects. He spoke of the surrender of the Constellation only once, to say:

"I knew there could be only Ragnarok in this section of space. I had to order four thousand people to go like sheep to what was to be their place of execution so that four thousand more could live as slaves. That was my last act as an officer."

Prentiss suspected that Lake found it impossible not to blame himself subconsciously for what circumstances had forced him to do. It was irrational—but conscientious men were quite often a little irrational in their sense of responsibility.

Lake had two subleaders: a genial, red-haired man named Ben Barber, who would have been a farmer on Athena but who made a good subleader on Ragnarok; and a lithe, cat-like man named Karl Schroeder.

Schroeder claimed to be twenty-four but not even the scars on his face could make him look more than twenty-one. He smiled often, a little too often. Prentiss had seen smiles like that before. Schroeder was the type who could smile while he killed a man—and he probably had.

But, if Schroeder was a born fighter and perhaps killer, they were characteristics that he expended entirely upon the prowlers. He was Lake's right hand man; a deadly marksman and utterly without fear.

One evening, when Lake had given Schroeder some instructions concerning the next day's activities, Schroeder answered him with the half-mocking smile and the words, "I'll see that it's done, Commander."

27

"Not 'Commander,'" Lake said. "I—all of us—left our ranks, titles and honors on the Constellation. The past is dead for us."

"I see," Schroeder said. The smile faded away and he looked into Lake's eyes as he asked, "And what about our past dishonors, disgraces and such?"

"They were left on the Constellation, too," Lake said. "If anyone wants dishonor he'll have to earn it all over again."

"That sounds fair," Schroeder said. "That sounds as fair as anyone could ever ask for."

He turned away and Prentiss saw what he had noticed before: Schroeder's black hair was coming out light brown at the roots. It was a color that would better match his light complexion and it was the color of hair that a man named Schrader, wanted by the police on Venus, had had.

Hair could be dyed, identification cards could be forged—but it was all something Prentiss did not care to pry into until and if Schroeder gave him reason to. Schroeder was a hard and dangerous man, despite his youth, and sometimes men of that type, when the chips were down, exhibited a higher sense of duty than the soft men who spoke piously of respect for Society—and then were afraid to face danger to protect the society and the people they claimed to respect.

A lone prowler came on the eleventh night following the wall's completion. It came silently, in the dead of night, and it learned how to reach in and tear apart the leather lashings that held the pointed stakes in place and then jerk the stakes out of their sockets. It was seen as it was removing the third stake—which would have made a large enough opening for it to come through—and shot. It fell back and managed to escape into the woods, although staggering and bleeding.

The next night the stockade was attacked by dozens of prowlers who simultaneously began removing the pointed stakes in the same manner employed by the prowler of the night before. Their attack was turned back with heavy losses on both sides and with a dismayingly large expenditure of precious ammunition.

There could be no doubt about how the band of prowlers had

28

learned to remove the stakes: the prowler of the night before had told them before it died. It was doubtful that the prowlers had a spoken language, but they had some means of communication. They worked together and they were highly intelligent, probably about halfway between dog and man.

The prowlers were going to be an enemy even more formidable than Prentiss had thought.

The missing stakes were replaced the next day and the others were tied down more securely. Once again the camp was prowler proof—but only for so long as armed guards patrolled inside the walls to kill attacking prowlers during the short time it would take them to remove the stakes.

The hunting parties suffered unusually heavy losses from prowler attacks that day and that evening, as the guards patrolled inside the walls, Lake said to Prentiss:

"The prowlers are so damnably persistent. It isn't that they're hungry—they don't kill us to eat us. They don't have any reason to kill us—they just hate us."

"They have a reason," Prentiss said. "They're doing the same thing we're doing: fighting for survival."

Lake's pale brows lifted in question.

"The prowlers are the rulers of Ragnarok," Prentiss said. "They fought their way up here, as men did on Earth, until they're master of every creature on their world. Even of the unicorns and swamp crawlers. But now we've come and they're intelligent enough to know that we're accustomed to being the dominant species, ourselves.

"There can't be two dominant species on the same world—and they know it. Men or prowlers—in the end one is going to have to go down before the other."

"I suppose you're right," Lake said. He looked at the guards, a fourth of them already reduced to bows and arrows that they had not yet had time to learn how to use. "If we win the battle for supremacy it will be a long fight, maybe over a period of centuries. And if the prowlers win—it may all be over within a year or two."

29

The giant blue star that was the other component of Ragnarok's binary grew swiftly in size as it preceded the yellow sun farther each morning. When summer came the blue star would be a sun as hot as the yellow sun and Ragnarok would be between them. The yellow sun would burn the land by day and the blue sun would sear it by the night that would not be night. Then would come the brief fall, followed by the long, frozen winter when the yellow sun would shine pale and cold, far to the south, and the blue sun would be a star again, two hundred and fifty million miles away and invisible behind the cold yellow sun.

The Hell Fever lessened with the completion of the shelters but it still killed each day. Chiara and his helpers worked with unfaltering determination to find a cure for it but the cure, if there was one, eluded them. The graves in the cemetery were forty long by forty wide and more were added each day. To all the fact became grimly obvious: they were swiftly dying out and they had yet to face Ragnarok at its worst.

The old survival instincts asserted themselves and there were marriages among the younger ones. One of the first to marry was Julia.

She stopped to talk to Prentiss one evening. She still wore the red skirt, now faded and patched, but her face was tired and thoughtful and no longer bold.

"Is it true, John," she asked, "that only a few of us might be able to have children here and that most of us who tried to have children in this gravity would die for it?"

"It's true," he said. "But you already knew that when you married."

"Yes ... I knew it." There was a little silence. "All my life I've had fun and done as I pleased. The human race didn't need me and we both knew it. But now—none of us can be apart from the others or be afraid of anything. If we're selfish and afraid there will come a time when the last of us will die and there will be nothing on Ragnarok to show we were ever here.

"I don't want it to end like that. I want there to be children, to live after we're gone. So I'm going to try to have a child. I'm not afraid and I won't be."

30

When he did not reply at once she said, almost self-consciously, "Coming from me that all sounds a little silly, I suppose."

"It sounds wise and splendid, Julia," he said, "and it's what I thought you were going to say."

Full spring came and the vegetation burst into leaf and bud and bloom, quickly, for its growth instincts knew in their mindless way how short was the time to grow and reproduce before the brown death of summer came. The prowlers were suddenly gone one day, to follow the spring north, and for a week men could walk and work outside the stockade without the protection of armed guards.

Then the new peril appeared, the one they had not expected: the unicorns.

The stockade wall was a blue-black rectangle behind them and the blue star burned with the brilliance of a dozen moons, lighting the woods in blue shadow and azure light. Prentiss and the hunter walked a little in front of the two riflemen, winding to keep in the starlit glades.

"It was on the other side of the next grove of trees," the hunter said in a low voice. "Fred was getting ready to bring in the rest of the woods goat. He shouldn't have been more than ten minutes behind me—and it's been over an hour."

They rounded the grove of trees. At first it seemed there was nothing before them but the empty, grassy glade. Then they saw it lying on the ground no more than twenty feet in front of them.

It was—it had been—a man. He was broken and stamped into hideous shapelessness and something had torn off his arms.

For a moment there was dead silence, then the hunter whispered, "What did that?"

The answer came in a savage, squealing scream and the pound of cloven hooves. A formless shadow beside the trees materialized into a monstrous charging bulk; a thing like a gigantic gray bull, eight feet tall at the shoulders, with the tusked, snarling head of a boar and the starlight glinting along the curving, vicious length of its single horn.

31

"Unicorn!" Prentiss said, and jerked up his rifle.

The rifles cracked in a ragged volley. The unicorn squealed in fury and struck the hunter, catching him on its horn and hurling him thirty feet. One of the riflemen went down under the unicorn's hooves, his cry ending almost as soon as it began.

The unicorn ripped the sod in deep furrows as it whirled back to Prentiss and the remaining rifleman; not turning in the manner of four-footed beasts of Earth but rearing and spinning on its hind feet. It towered above them as it whirled, the tip of its horn fifteen feet above the ground and its hooves swinging around like great clubs.

Prentiss shot again, his sights on what he hoped would be a vital area, and the rifleman shot an instant later.

The shots went true. The unicorn's swing brought it on around but it collapsed, falling to the ground with jarring heaviness.

"We got it!" the rifleman said. "We——"

It half scrambled to its feet and made a noise; a call that went out through the night like the blast of a mighty trumpet. Then it dropped back to the ground, to die while its call was still echoing from the nearer hills.

From the east came an answering trumpet blast; a trumpeting that was sounded again from the south and from the north. Then there came a low and muffled drumming, like the pounding of thousands of hooves.

The rifleman's face was blue-white in the starlight. "The others are coming—we'll have to run for it!"

He turned, and began to run toward the distant bulk of the stockade.

"No!" Prentiss commanded, quick and harsh. "Not the stockade!"

The rifleman kept running, seeming not to hear him in his panic. Prentiss called to him once more:

"Not the stockade—you'll lead the unicorns into it!"

32

Again the rifleman seemed not to hear him.

The unicorns were coming in sight, converging in from the north and east and south, the rumble of their hooves swelling to a thunder that filled the night. The rifleman would reach the stockade only a little ahead of them and they would go through the wall as though it had been made of paper.

For a little while the area inside the stockade would be filled with dust, with the squealing of the swirling, charging unicorns and the screams of the dying. Those inside the stockade would have no chance whatever of escaping. Within two minutes it would be over, the last child would have been found among the shattered shelters and trampled into lifeless shapelessness in the bloody ground.

Within two minutes all human life on Ragnarok would be gone.

There was only one thing for him to do.

He dropped to one knee so his aim would be steady and the sights of his rifle caught the running man's back. He pressed the trigger and the rifle cracked viciously as it bucked against his shoulder.

The man spun and fell hard to the ground. He twisted, to raise himself up a little and look back, his face white and accusing and unbelieving.

"You shot me!"

Then he fell forward and lay without moving.

Prentiss turned back to face the unicorns and to look at the trees in the nearby grove. He saw what he already knew, they were young trees and too small to offer any escape for him. There was no place to run, no place to hide.

There was nothing he could do but wait; nothing he could do but stand in the blue starlight and watch the devil's herd pound toward him and think, in the last moments of his life, how swiftly and unexpectedly death could come to man on Ragnarok.

The unicorns held the Rejects prisoners in their stockade the rest of the night and all the next day. Lake had seen the shooting of the rifleman and had watched the unicorn herd kill John Prentiss and then trample the dead rifleman.

He had already given the order to build a quick series of fires around the inside of the stockade walls when the unicorns paused to tear their victims to pieces; grunting and squealing in triumph as bones crushed between their teeth and they flung the pieces to one side.

The fires were started and green wood was thrown on them, to make them smoulder and smoke for as long as possible. Then the unicorns were coming on to the stockade and every person inside it went into the concealment of the shelters.

Lake had already given his last order: There would be absolute quiet until and if the unicorns left; a quiet that would be enforced with fist or club wherever necessary.

The unicorns were still outside when morning came. The fires could not be refueled; the sight of a man moving inside the stockade would bring the entire herd charging through. The hours dragged by, the smoke from the dying fires dwindled to thin streamers. The unicorns grew increasingly bolder and suspicious, crowding closer to the walls and peering through the openings between the rails.

The sun was setting when one of the unicorns trumpeted; a sound different from that of the call to battle. The others threw up their heads to listen, then they turned and drifted away. Within minutes the entire herd was gone out of sight through the woods, toward the north.

Lake waited and watched until he was sure the unicorns were gone for good. Then he ordered the All Clear given and hurried to the south wall, to look down across the barren valley and hope he would not see what he expected to see.

Barber came up behind him, to sigh with relief. "That was close. It's hard to make so many people stay absolutely quiet for hour after hour. Especially the children—they don't understand."

"We'll have to leave," Lake said.

"Leave?" Barber asked. "We can make this stockade strong enough to hold out unicorns."

34

"Look to the south," Lake told him.

Barber did so and saw what Lake had already seen; a broad, low cloud of dust moving slowly toward them.

"Another herd of unicorns," Lake said. "John didn't know they migrated—the Dunbar Expedition wasn't here long enough to learn that. There'll be herd after herd coming through and no time for us to strengthen the walls. We'll have to leave tonight."

Preparations were made for the departure; preparations that consisted mainly of providing each person with as much in the way of food or supplies as he or she could carry. In the 1.5 gravity, that was not much.

They left when the blue star rose. They filed out through the northern gate and the rear guard closed it behind them. There was almost no conversation among them. Some of them turned to take a last look at what had been the only home they had ever known on Ragnarok, then they all faced forward again, to the northwest, where the foothills of the plateau might offer them sanctuary.

They found their sanctuary on the second day; a limestone ridge honey-combed with caves. Men were sent back at once to carry the food and supplies left in the stockade to the new home.

They returned, to report that the second herd of unicorns had broken down the walls and ripped the interior of the stockade into wreckage. Much of the food and supplies had been totally destroyed.

Lake sent them back twice more to bring everything, down to the last piece of bent metal or torn cloth. They would find uses for all of it in the future.

The cave system was extensive, containing room for several times their number. The deeper portions of the caves could not be lived in until ventilation ducts were made, but the outer caves were more than sufficient in number. Work was begun to clear them of fallen rubble, to pry down all loose material overhead and to level the floors. A spring came out of the ridge not far from the caves and the approach to the caves was so narrow and steep that unicorns could

35

scramble up it only with difficulty and one at a time. And should they ever reach the natural terrace in front of the caves they would be too large to enter and could do no more than stand outside and make targets of themselves for the bowmen within.

Anders was in charge of making the caves livable, his working force restricted almost entirely to women and children. Lake sent Barber out, with a small detachment of men, to observe the woods goats and learn what plants they ate. And then learn, by experimenting, if such plants could be safely eaten by humans.

The need for salt would be tremendously increased when summer came. Having once experienced a saltless two weeks in the desert Lake doubted that any of them could survive without it. All hunting parties, as well as Barber's party, were ordered to investigate all deposits that might contain salt as well as any stream or pond that was white along the banks.

The hunting parties were of paramount importance and they were kept out to the limits of their endurance. Every man physically able to do so accompanied them. Those who could not kill game could carry it back to the caves. There was no time to spare; already the unicorns were decreasing in numbers and the woods goats were ranging farther and farther north.

At the end of twenty days Lake went in search of Barber and his party, worried about them. Their mission was one that could be as dangerous as any hunting trip. There was no proof that humans and Ragnarok creatures were so similar as to guarantee that food for one might not be poison for the other. It was a very necessary mission, however; dried meat, alone, would bring grave deficiency diseases during the summer which dried herbs and fruits would help prevent.

When he located Barber's party he found Barber lying under a tree, pale and weak from his latest experiment but recovering.

"I was the guinea pig yesterday," Barber said. "Some little purple berries that the woods goats nibble at sometimes, maybe to get a touch of some certain vitamin or something. I ate too many, I guess, because they hit my heart like the kick of a mule."

"Did you find anything at all encouraging?" Lake asked.

36

"We found four different herbs that are the most violent cathartics you ever dreamed of. And a little silvery fern that tastes like vanilla flavored candy and paralyzes you stiff as a board on the third swallow. It's an hour before you come back out of it.

"But on the good side we found three different kinds of herbs that seem to be all right. We've been digging them up and hanging them in the trees to dry."

Lake tried the edible herbs and found them to be something like spinach in taste. There was a chance they might contain the vitamins and minerals needed. Since the hunting parties were living exclusively on meat he would have to point out the edible herbs to all of them so they would know what to eat should any of them feel the effects of diet deficiency.

He traveled alone as he visited the various hunting parties, finding such travel to be safer each day as the dwindling of the unicorns neared the vanishing point. It was a safety he did not welcome; it meant the last of the game would be gone north long before sufficient meat was taken.

None of the hunting parties could report good luck. The woods goats, swift and elusive at best, were vanishing with the unicorns. The last cartridge had been fired and the bowmen, while improving all the time, were far from expert. The unicorns, which should have been their major source of meat, were invulnerable to arrows unless shot at short range in the side of the neck just behind the head. And at short range the unicorns invariably charged and presented no such target.

He made the long, hard climb up the plateau's southern face, to stand at last on top. It was treeless, a flat, green table that stretched to the north for as far as he could see. A mountain range, still capped with snow, lay perhaps a hundred miles to the northwest; in the distance it looked like a white, low-lying cloud on the horizon. No other mountains or hills marred the endless sweep of the high plain.

The grass was thick and here and there were little streams of water produced by the recently melted snow. It was a paradise land for the herbivores of Ragnarok but for men it was a harsh, forbidding place. At that elevation the air was so thin that only a moderate amount of exertion made the heart and lungs labor painfully. Hard and prolonged exertion would be impossible.

It seemed unlikely that men could hunt and dare unicorn attacks at such an elevation but two hunting parties were ahead of him; one under the grim Craig and one under the reckless Schroeder, both parties stripped down to the youngest, strongest men among all the Rejects.

He found Schroeder early one morning, leading his hunters toward a small band of woods goats. Two unicorns were grazing in between and the hunters were swinging downwind from them. Schroeder saw him coming and walked back a little way to meet him.

"Welcome to our breathtaking land," Schroeder greeted him. "How are things going with the rest of the hunting parties?"

Schroeder was gaunt and there was weariness beneath his still lithe movements. His whiskers were an untamed sorrel bristling and across his cheekbone was the ugly scar of a half healed wound. Another gash was ripped in his arm and something had battered one ear. He reminded Lake of a battle-scarred, indomitable tomcat who would never, for as long as he lived, want to relinquish the joy of conflict and danger.

"So far," he answered, "you and Craig are the only parties to manage to tackle the plateau."

He asked about Schroeder's luck and learned it had been much better than that of the others due to killing three unicorns by a method Schroeder had thought of.

"Since the bowmen have to be to one side of the unicorns to kill them," Schroeder said, "it only calls for a man to be the decoy and let the unicorns chase him between the hidden bowmen. If there's no more than one or two unicorns and if the decoy doesn't have to run very far and if the bowmen don't miss it works well."

"Judging from your beat-up condition," Lake said, "you must have been the decoy every time."

"Well——" Schroeder shrugged his shoulders. "It was my idea."

"I've been wondering about another way to get in shots at close

38

range," Lake said. "Take the skin of a woods goat, give it the original shape as near as possible, and a bowman inside it might be able to fake a grazing woods goat until he got the shot he wanted.

"The unicorns might never suspect where the arrows came from," he concluded. "And then, of course, they might."

"I'll try it before the day is over, on those two unicorns over there," Schroeder said. "At this elevation and in this gravity my own method is just a little bit rough on a man."

Lake found Craig and his men several miles to the west, all of them gaunt and bearded as Schroeder had been.

"We've had hell," Craig said. "It seems that every time we spot a few woods goats there will be a dozen unicorns in between. If only we had rifles for the unicorns...."

Lake told him of the plan to hide under woods goats' skins and of the decoy system used by Schroeder.

"Maybe we won't have to use Schroeder's method," he said. "We'll see if the other works—I'll give it the first try."

This he was not to do. Less than an hour later one of the men who helped dry the meat and carry it to the caves returned to report the camp stricken by a strange, sudden malady that was killing a hundred a day. Dr. Chiara, who had collapsed while driving himself on to care for the sick, was sure it was a deficiency disease. Anders was down with it, helpless, and Bemmon had assumed command; setting up daily work quotas for those still on their feet and refusing to heed Chiara's requests concerning treatment of the disease.

Lake made the trip back to the caves in a fraction of the length of time it had taken him to reach the plateau, walking until he was ready to drop and then pausing only for an hour or two of rest. He spotted Barber's camp when coming down off the plateau and he swung to one side, to tell Barber to have a supply of the herbs sent to the caves at once.

He reached the caves, to find half the camp in bed and the other half dragging about listlessly at the tasks given them by Bemmon.

39

Anders was in grave condition, too weak to rise, and Dr. Chiara was dying.

He squatted down beside Chiara's pallet and knew there could be no hope for him. On Chiara's pale face and in his eyes was the shadow of his own foreknowledge.

"I finally saw what it was"—Chiara's words were very low, hard to hear—"and I told Bemmon what to do. It's a deficiency disease, complicated by the gravity into some form not known on Earth."

He stopped to rest and Lake waited.

"Beri-beri—pellagra—we had deficiency diseases on Earth. But none so fatal—so quickly. I told Bemmon—ration out fruits and vegetables to everybody. Hurry—or it will be too late."

Again he stopped to rest, the last vestige of color gone from his face.

"And you?" Lake asked, already knowing the answer.

"For me—too late. I kept thinking of viruses—should have seen the obvious sooner. Just like——"

His lips turned up a little at the corners and the Chiara of the dead past smiled for the last time at Lake.

"Just like a damned fool intern...."

That was all, then, and the chamber was suddenly very quiet. Lake stood up to leave, and to speak the words that Chiara could never hear:

"We're going to need you and miss you—Doctor."

He found Bemmon in the food storage cavern, supervising the work of two teen-age boys with critical officiousness although he was making no move to help them. At sight of Lake he hurried forward, the ingratiating smile sliding across his face.

"I'm glad you're back," he said. "I had to take charge when Anders got sick and he had everything in such a mess. I've been working

40

day and night to undo his mistakes and get the work properly under way again."

Lake looked at the two thin-faced boys who had taken advantage of the opportunity to rest. They leaned wearily against the heavy pole table Bemmon had had them moving, their eyes already dull with the incipient sickness and watching him in mute appeal.

"Have you obeyed Chiara's order?" he asked.

"Ah—no," Bemmon said. "I felt it best to ignore it."

"Why?" Lake asked.

"It would be a senseless waste of our small supply of fruit and vegetable foods to give them to people already dying. I'm afraid"— the ingratiating smile came again—"we've been letting him exercise an authority he isn't entitled to. He's really hardly more than a medical student and his diagnoses are only guesses."

"He's dead," Lake said flatly. "His last order will be carried out."

He looked from the two tired boys to Bemmon, contrasting their thinness and weariness with the way Bemmon's paunch still bulged outward and his jowls still sagged with their load of fat.

"I'll send West down to take over in here," he said to Bemmon. "You come with me. You and I seem to be the only two in good health here and there's plenty of work for us to do."

The fawning expression vanished from Bemmon's face. "I see," he said. "Now that I've turned Anders's muddle into organization, you'll hand my authority over to another of your favorites and demote me back to common labor?"

"Setting up work quotas for sick and dying people isn't organization," Lake said. He spoke to the two boys, "Both of you go lie down. West will find someone else." Then to Bemmon, "Come with me. We're both going to work at common labor."

They passed by the cave where Bemmon slept. Two boys were just going into it, carrying armloads of dried grass to make a mattress under Bemmon's pallet. They moved slowly, heavily. Like the two

41

boys in the food storage cave they were dull-eyed with the beginning of the sickness.

Lake stopped, to look more closely into the cave and verify something else he thought he had seen: Bemmon had discarded the prowler skins on his bed and in their place were soft wool blankets; perhaps the only unpatched blankets the Rejects possessed.

"Go back to your caves," he said to the boys. "Go to bed and rest."

He looked at Bemmon. Bemmon's eyes flickered away, refusing to meet his.

"What few blankets we have are for babies and the very youngest children," he said. His tone was coldly unemotional but he could not keep his fists from clenching at his sides. "You will return them at once and sleep on animal skins, as all the men and women do. And if you want grass for a mattress you will carry it yourself, as even the young children do."

Bemmon made no answer, his face a sullen red and hatred shining in the eyes that still refused to meet Lake's.

"Gather up the blankets and return them," Lake said. "Then come on up to the central cave. We have a lot of work to do."

He could feel Bemmon's gaze burning against his back as he turned away and he thought of what John Prentiss had once said:

"I know he's no good but he never has guts enough to go quite far enough to give me an excuse to whittle him down."

Barber's men arrived the next day, burdened with dried herbs. These were given to the seriously ill as a supplement to the ration of fruit and vegetable foods and were given, alone, to those not yet sick. Then came the period of waiting; of hoping that it was all not too late and too little.

A noticeable change for the better began on the second day. A week went by and the sick were slowly, steadily, improving. The not-quite-sick were already back to normal health. There was no longer any doubt: the Ragnarok herbs would prevent a recurrence of the disease.

It was, Lake thought, all so simple once you knew what to do. Hundreds had died, Chiara among them, because they did not have a common herb that grew at a slightly higher elevation. Not a single life would have been lost if he could have looked a week into the future and had the herbs found and taken to the caves that much sooner.

But the disease had given no warning of its coming. Nothing, on Ragnarok, ever seemed to give warning before it killed.

Another week went by and hunters began to trickle in, gaunt and exhausted, to report all the game going north up the plateau and not a single creature left below. They were the ones who had tried and failed to withstand the high elevation of the plateau. Only two out of three hunters returned among those who had challenged the plateau. They had tried, all of them, to the best of their ability and the limits of their endurance.

The blue star was by then a small sun and the yellow sun blazed hotter each day. Grass began to brown and wither on the hillsides as the days went by and Lake knew summer was very near. The last hunting party, but for Craig's and Schroeder's, returned. They had very little meat but they brought with them a large quantity of something almost as important: salt.

They had found a deposit of it in an almost inaccessible region of cliffs and canyons. "Not even the woods goats can get in there," Stevens, the leader of that party, said. "If the salt was in an accessible place there would have been a salt lick there and goats in plenty."

"If woods goats care for salt the way Earth animals do," Lake said. "When fall comes we'll make a salt lick and find out."

Two more weeks went by and Craig and Schroeder returned with their surviving hunters. They had followed the game to the eastern end of the snow-capped mountain range but there the migration had drawn away from them, traveling farther each day than they could travel. They had almost waited too long before turning back: the grass at the southern end of the plateau was turning brown and the streams were dry. They got enough water, barely, by digging seep holes in the dry stream beds.

Lake's method of stalking unicorns under the concealment of a

43

woods goat skin had worked well only a few times. After that the unicorns learned to swing downwind from any lone woods goats. If they smelled a man inside the goat skin they charged him and killed him.

With the return of the last hunters everything was done that could be done in preparation for summer. Inventory was taken of the total food supply and it was even smaller than Lake had feared. It would be far from enough to last until fall brought the game back from the north and he instituted rationing much stricter than before.

The heat increased as the yellow sun blazed hotter and the blue sun grew larger. Each day the vegetation was browner and a morning came when Lake could see no green wherever he looked.

They numbered eleven hundred and ten that morning, out of what had so recently been four thousand. Eleven hundred and ten thin, hungry scarecrows who, already, could do nothing more than sit listlessly in the shade and wait for the hell that was coming. He thought of the food supply, so pitifully small, and of the months it would have to last. He saw the grim, inescapable future for his charges: famine. There was nothing he could do to prevent it. He could only try to forestall complete starvation for all by cutting rations to the bare existence level.

And that would be bare existence for the stronger of them. The weaker were already doomed.

He had them all gather in front of the caves that evening when the terrace was in the shadow of the ridge. He stood before them and spoke to them:

"All of you know we have only a fraction of the amount of food we need to see us through the summer. Tomorrow the present ration will be cut in half. That will be enough to live on, just barely. If that cut isn't made the food supply will be gone long before fall and all of us will die.

"If anyone has any food of any kind it must be turned in to be added to the total supply. Some of you may have thought of your children and kept a little hidden for them. I can understand why you should do that—but you must turn it in. There may possibly be some who hid food for themselves, personally. If so, I give them the first and

44

last warning: turn it in tonight. If any hidden cache of food is found in the future the one who hid it will be regarded as a traitor and murderer.

"All of you, but for the children, will go into the chamber next to the one where the food is stored. Each of you—and there will be no exceptions regardless of how innocent you are—will carry a bulkily folded cloth or garment. Each of you will go into the chamber alone. There will be no one in there. You will leave the food you have folded in the cloth, if any, and go out the other exit and back to your caves. No one will ever know whether the cloth you carried contained food or not. No one will ever ask.

"Our survival on this world, if we are to survive at all, can be only by working and sacrificing together. There can be no selfishness. What any of you may have done in the past is of no consequence. Tonight we start anew. From now on we trust one another without reserve.

"There will be one punishment for any who betray that trust—death."

Anders set the example by being the first to carry a folded cloth into the cave. Of them all, Lake heard later, only Bemmon voiced any real indignation; warning all those in his section of the line that the order was the first step toward outright dictatorship and a police-and-spy system in which Lake and the other leaders would deprive them all of freedom and dignity. Bemmon insisted upon exhibiting the emptiness of the cloth he carried; an action that, had he succeeded in persuading the others to follow his example, would have mercilessly exposed those who did have food they were returning.

But no one followed Bemmon's example and no harm was done. As for Lake, he had worries on his mind of much greater importance than Bemmon's enmity.

The weeks dragged by, each longer and more terrible to endure than the one before it as the heat steadily increased. Summer solstice arrived and there was no escape from the heat, even in the deepest caves. There was no night; the blue sun rose in the east as the yellow sun set in the west. There was no life of any kind to be seen, not

45

even an insect. Nothing moved across the burned land but the swirling dust devils and shimmering, distorted mirages.

The death rate increased with appalling swiftness. The small supply of canned and dehydrated milk, fruit and vegetables was reserved exclusively for the children but it was far insufficient in quantity. The Ragnarok herbs prevented any recurrence of the fatal deficiency disease but they provided virtually no nourishment to help fight the heat and gravity. The stronger of the children lay wasted and listless on their pallets while the ones not so strong died each day.

Each day thin and hollow-eyed mothers would come to plead with him to save their children. "... it would take so little to save his life.... Please—before it's too late...."

But there was so little food left and the time was yet so long until fall would bring relief from the famine that he could only answer each of them with a grim and final "No."

And watch the last hope flicker and die in their eyes and watch them turn away, to go and sit for the last hours beside their children.

Bemmon became increasingly irritable and complaining as the rationing and heat made existence a misery; insisting that Lake and the others were to blame for the food shortage, that their hunting efforts had been bungling and faint-hearted. And he implied, without actually saying so, that Lake and the others had forbidden him to go near the food chamber because they did not want a competent, honest man to check up on what they were doing.

There were six hundred and three of them the blazing afternoon when the girl, Julia, could stand his constant, vindictive, fault-finding no longer. Lake heard about it shortly afterward, the way she had turned on Bemmon in a flare of temper she could control no longer and said:

"Whenever your mouth is still you can hear the children who are dying today—but you don't care. All you can think of is yourself. You claim Lake and the others were cowards—but you didn't dare hunt with them. You keep insinuating that they're cheating us and eating more than we are—but your belly is the only one that has any fat left on it——"

She never completed the sentence. Bemmon's face turned livid in

46

sudden, wild fury and he struck her, knocking her against the rock wall so hard that she slumped unconscious to the ground.

"She's a liar!" he panted, glaring at the others. "She's a rotten liar and anybody who repeats what she said will get what she got!"

When Lake learned of what had happened he did not send for Bemmon at once. He wondered why Bemmon's reaction had been so quick and violent and there seemed to be only one answer:

Bemmon's belly was still a little fat. There could be but one way he could have kept it so.

He summoned Craig, Schroeder, Barber and Anders. They went to the chamber where Bemmon slept and there, almost at once, they found his cache. He had it buried under his pallet and hidden in cavities along the walls; dried meat, dried fruits and milk, canned vegetables. It was an amount amazingly large and many of the items had presumably been exhausted during the deficiency disease attack.

"It looks," Schroeder said, "like he didn't waste any time feathering his nest when he made himself leader."

The others said nothing but stood with grim, frozen faces, waiting for Lake's next action.

"Bring Bemmon," Lake said to Craig.

Craig returned with him two minutes later. Bemmon stiffened at the sight of his unearthed cache and color drained away from his face.

"Well?" Lake asked.

"I didn't"—Bemmon swallowed—"I didn't know it was there." And then quickly, "You can't prove I put it there. You can't prove you didn't just now bring it in yourselves to frame me."

Lake stared at Bemmon, waiting. The others watched Bemmon as Lake was doing and no one spoke. The silence deepened and Bemmon began to sweat as he tried to avoid their eyes. He looked again at the damning evidence and his defiance broke.

"It—if I hadn't taken it it would have been wasted on people who

47

were dying," he said. He wiped at his sweating face. "I won't ever do it again—I swear I won't."

Lake spoke to Craig. "You and Barber take him to the lookout point."

"What——" Bemmon's protest was cut off as Craig and Barber took him by the arms and walked him swiftly away.

Lake turned to Anders. "Get a rope," he ordered.

Anders paled a little. "A—rope?"

"What else does he deserve?"

"Nothing," Anders said. "Not—not after what he did."

On the way out they passed the place where Julia lay. Bemmon had knocked her against the wall with such force that a sharp projection of rock had cut a deep gash in her forehead. A woman was wiping the blood from her face and she lay limply, still unconscious; a frail shadow of the bold girl she had once been with the new life she would try to give them an almost unnoticeable little bulge in her starved thinness.

The lookout point was an outjutting spur of the ridge, six hundred feet from the caves and in full view of them. A lone tree stood there, its dead limbs thrust like white arms through the brown foliage of the limbs that still lived. Craig and Barber waited under the tree, Bemmon between them. The lowering sun shone hot and bright on Bemmon's face as he squinted back toward the caves at the approach of Lake and the other two.

He twisted to look at Barber. "What is it—why did you bring me here?" There was the tremor of fear in his voice. "What are you going to do to me?"

Barber did not answer and Bemmon turned back toward Lake. He saw the rope in Anders' hand and his face went white with comprehension.

"No!"

48

He threw himself back with a violence that almost tore him loose. "No—no!"

Schroeder stepped forward to help hold him and Lake took the rope from Anders. He fashioned a noose in it while Bemmon struggled and made panting, animal sounds, his eyes fixed in horrified fascination on the rope.

When the noose was finished he threw the free end of the rope over the white limb above Bemmon. He released the noose and Barber caught it, to draw it snug around Bemmon's neck.

Bemmon stopped struggling then and sagged weakly. For a moment it appeared that he would faint. Then he worked his mouth soundlessly until words came:

"You won't—you can't—really hang me?"

Lake spoke to him:

"We're going to hang you. What you stole would have saved the lives of ten children. You've watched the children cry because they were so hungry and you've watched them become too weak to cry or care any more. You've watched them die each day and each night you've secretly eaten the food that was supposed to be theirs.

"We're going to hang you, for the murder of children and the betrayal of our trust in you. If you have anything to say, say it now."

"You can't! I had a right to live—to eat what would have been wasted on dying people!" Bemmon twisted to appeal to the ones who held him, his words quick and ragged with hysteria. "You can't hang me—I don't want to die!"

Craig answered him, with a smile that was like the thin snarl of a wolf:

"Neither did two of my children."

Lake nodded to Craig and Schroeder, not waiting any longer. They stepped back to seize the free end of the rope and Bemmon screamed at what was coming, tearing loose from the grip of Barber.

49

Then his scream was abruptly cut off as he was jerked into the air. There was a cracking sound and he kicked spasmodically, his head setting grotesquely to one side.

Craig and Schroeder and Barber watched him with hard, expressionless faces but Anders turned quickly away, to be suddenly and violently sick.

"He was the first to betray us," Lake said. "Snub the rope and leave him to swing there. If there are any others like him, they'll know what to expect."

The blue sun rose as they went back to the caves. Behind them Bemmon swung and twirled aimlessly on the end of the rope. Two long, pale shadows swung and twirled with him; a yellow one to the west and a blue one to the east.

Bemmon was buried the next day. Someone cursed his name and someone spit on his grave and then he was part of the dead past as they faced the suffering ahead of them.

Julia recovered, although she would always wear a ragged scar on her forehead. Anders, who had worked closely with Chiara and was trying to take his place, quieted her fears by assuring her that the baby she carried was still too small for there to be much danger of the fall causing her to lose it.

Three times during the next month the wind came roaring down out of the northwest, bringing a gray dust that filled the sky and enveloped the land in a hot, smothering gloom through which the suns could not be seen.

Once black clouds gathered in the distance, to pour out a cloudburst. The 1.5 gravity gave the wall of water that swept down the canyon a far greater force and velocity than it would have had on Earth and boulders the size of small houses were tossed into the air and shattered into fragments. But all the rain fell upon the one small area and not a drop fell at the caves.

One single factor was in their favor and but for it they could not have survived such intense, continual heat: there was no humidity. Water evaporated quickly in the hot, dry air and sweat glands operated at the highest possible degree of efficiency. As a result they drank enormous quantities of water—the average adult needed five gallons a day. All canvas had been converted into water bags and the same principle of cooling-by-evaporation gave them water that was only warm instead of sickeningly hot as it would otherwise have been.

But despite the lack of humidity the heat was still far more intense than any on Earth. It never ceased, day or night, never let them have a moment's relief. There was a limit to how long human flesh could bear up under it, no matter how valiant the will. Each day the toll of those who had reached that limit was greater, like a swiftly rising tide.

There were three hundred and forty of them, when the first rain came; the rain that meant the end of summer. The yellow sun moved southward and the blue sun shrank steadily. Grass grew again and the woods goats returned, with them the young that had been born in the north, already half the size of their mothers.

For a while there was meat, and green herbs. Then the prowlers came, to make hunting dangerous. Females with pups were seen but always at a great distance as though the prowlers, like humans, took no chances with the lives of their children.

The unicorns came close behind the first prowlers, their young amazingly large and already weaned. Hunting became doubly dangerous then but the bowmen, through necessity, were learning how to use their bows with increasing skill and deadliness.

A salt lick for the woods goats was hopefully tried, although Lake felt dubious about it. They learned that salt was something the woods goats could either take or leave alone. And when hunters were in the vicinity they left it alone.

The game was followed for many miles to the south. The hunters returned the day the first blizzard came roaring and screaming down over the edge of the plateau; the blizzard that marked the beginning of the long, frigid winter. By then they were prepared as best they could be. Wood had been carried in great quantities and the caves fitted with crude doors and a ventilation system. And they had meat—not as much as they would need but enough to prevent starvation.

Lake took inventory of the food supply when the last hunters returned and held check-up inventories at irregular and unannounced intervals. He found no shortages. He had expected none—Bemmon's grave had long since been obliterated by drifting snow but the rope still hung from the dead limb, the noose swinging and turning in the wind.

Anders had made a Ragnarok calendar that spring, from data given him by John Prentiss, and he had marked the corresponding Earth dates on it. By a coincidence, Christmas came near the middle of the winter. There would be the same rationing of food on Christmas day but little brown trees had been cut for the children and decorated with such ornaments as could be made from the materials at hand.

There was another blizzard roaring down off the plateau Christmas morning; a white death that thundered and howled outside the caves at a temperature of more than eighty degrees below zero. But inside the caves it was warm by the fires and under the little brown trees were toys that had been patiently whittled from wood or sewn from scraps of cloth and animal skins while the children slept. They were crude and humble toys but the pale, thin faces of the children were bright with delight when they beheld them.

There was the laughter of children at play, a sound that had not been heard for many months, and someone singing the old, old songs. For a few fleeting hours that day, for the first and last time on Ragnarok, there was the magic of an Earth Christmas.

That night a child was born to Julia, on a pallet of dried grass and prowler skins. She asked for her baby before she died and they let her have it.

"I wasn't afraid, was I?" she asked. "But I wish it wasn't so dark—I wish I could see my baby before I go."

They took the baby from her arms when she was gone and removed from it the blanket that had kept her from learning that her child was still-born.

There were two hundred and fifty of them when the first violent storms of spring came. By then eighteen children had been born. Sixteen were still-born, eight of them deformed by the gravity, but two were like any normal babies on Earth. There was only one

52

difference: the 1.5 gravity did not seem to affect them as much as it had the Earth-born babies.

Lake, himself, married that spring; a tall, gray-eyed girl who had fought alongside the men the night of the storm when the prowlers broke into John Prentiss's camp. And Schroeder married, the last of them all to do so.

That spring Lake sent out two classes of bowmen: those who would use the ordinary short bow and those who would use the longbows he had had made that winter. According to history the English longbowmen of medieval times had been without equal in the range and accuracy of their arrows and such extra-powerful weapons should eliminate close range stalking of woods goats and afford better protection from unicorns.

The longbows worked so well that by mid-spring he could detach Craig and three others from the hunting and send them on a prospecting expedition. Prentiss had said Ragnarok was devoid of metals but there was the hope of finding small veins the Dunbar Expedition's instruments had not detected. They would have to find metal or else, in the end, they would go back into a flint axe stage.

Craig and his men returned when the blue star was a sun again and the heat was more than men could walk and work in. They had traveled hundreds of miles in their circuit and found no metals.

"I want to look to the south when fall comes," Craig said. "Maybe it will be different down there."

They did not face famine that summer as they had the first summer. The diet of meat and dried herbs was rough and plain but there was enough of it.

Full summer came and the land was again burned and lifeless. There was nothing to do but sit wearily in the shade and endure the heat, drawing what psychological comfort they could from the fact that summer solstice was past and the suns were creeping south again even though it would be many weeks before there was any lessening of the heat.

It was then, and by accident, that Lake discovered there was something wrong about the southward movement of the suns.

He was returning from the lookout that day and he realized it was exactly a year since he and the others had walked back to the caves while Bemmon swung on the limb behind them.

It was even the same time of day; the blue sun rising in the east behind him and the yellow sun bright in his face as it touched the western horizon before him. He remembered how the yellow sun had been like the front sight of a rifle, set in the deepest V notch of the western hills—

But now, exactly a year later, it was not in the V notch. It was on the north side of the notch.

He looked to the east, at the blue sun. It seemed to him that it, too, was farther north than it had been although with it he had no landmark to check by.

But there was no doubt about the yellow sun: it was going south, as it should at that time of year, but it was lagging behind schedule. The only explanation Lake could think of was one that would mean still another threat to their survival; perhaps greater than all the others combined.

The yellow sun dropped completely behind the north slope of the V notch and he went on to the caves. He found Craig and Anders, the only two who might know anything about Ragnarok's axial tilts, and told them what he had seen.

"I made the calendar from the data John gave me," Anders said. "The Dunbar men made observations and computed the length of Ragnarok's year—I don't think they would have made any mistakes."

"If they didn't," Lake said, "we're in for something."

Craig was watching him, closely, thoughtfully. "Like the Ice Ages of Earth?" he asked.

Lake nodded and Anders said, "I don't understand."

"Each year the north pole tilts toward the sun to give us summer and away from it to give us winter," Lake said. "Which, of course, you know. But there can be still another kind of axial tilt. On Earth

54

it occurs at intervals of thousands of years. The tilting that produces the summers and winters goes on as usual but as the centuries go by the summer tilt toward the sun grows less, the winter tilt away from it greater. The north pole leans farther and farther from the sun and ice sheets come down out of the north—an Ice Age. Then the north pole's progression away from the sun stops and the ice sheets recede as it tilts back toward the sun."

"I see," Anders said. "And if the same thing is happening here, we're going away from an ice age but at a rate thousands of times faster than on Earth."

"I don't know whether it's Ragnarok's tilt, alone, or if the orbits of the suns around each other add effects of their own over a period of years," Lake said. "The Dunbar Expedition wasn't here long enough to check up on anything like that."

"It seemed to me it was hotter this summer than last," Craig said. "Maybe only my imagination—but it won't be imagination in a few years if the tilt toward the sun continues."

"The time would come when we'd have to leave here," Lake said. "We'd have to go north up the plateau each spring. There's no timber there—nothing but grass and wind and thin air. We'd have to migrate south each fall."

"Yes ... migrate." Anders's face was old and weary in the harsh reflected light of the blue sun and his hair had turned almost white in the past year. "Only the young ones could ever adapt enough to go up the plateau to its north portion. The rest of us ... but we haven't many years, anyway. Ragnarok is for the young—and if they have to migrate back and forth like animals just to stay alive they will never have time to accomplish anything or be more than stone age nomads."

"I wish we could know how long the Big Summer will be that we're going into," Craig said. "And how long and cold the Big Winter, when Ragnarok tilts away from the sun. It wouldn't change anything—but I'd like to know."

"We'll start making and recording daily observations," Lake said. "Maybe the tilt will start back the other way before it's too late."

Fall seemed to come a little later that year. Craig went to the south as soon as the weather permitted but there were no minerals there; only the metal-barren hills dwindling in size until they became a prairie that sloped down and down toward the southern lowlands where all the creatures of Ragnarok spent the winter.

"I'll try again to the north when spring comes," Craig said. "Maybe that mountain on the plateau will have something."

Winter came, and Elaine died in giving him a son. The loss of Elaine was an unexpected blow; hurting more than he would ever have thought possible.

But he had a son ... and it was his responsibility to do whatever he could to insure the survival of his son and of the sons and daughters of all the others.

His outlook altered and he began to think of the future, not in terms of years to come but in terms of generations to come. Someday one of the young ones would succeed him as leader but the young ones would have only childhood memories of Earth. He was the last leader who had known Earth and the civilization of Earth as a grown man. What he did while he was leader would incline the destiny of a new race.

He would have to do whatever was possible for him to do and he would have to begin at once. The years left to him could not be many.

He was not alone; others in the caves had the same thoughts he had regarding the future even though none of them had any plan for accomplishing what they spoke of. West, who had held degrees in philosophy on Earth, said to Lake one night as they sat together by the fire:

"Have you noticed the way the children listen when the talk turns to what used to be on Earth, what might have been on Athena, and what would be if only we could find a way to escape from Ragnarok?"

"I've noticed," he said.

"These stories already contain the goal for the future generations,"

56

West went on. "Someday, somehow, they will go to Athena, to kill the Germs there and free the Terran slaves and reclaim Athena as their own."

He had listened to them talk of the interstellar flight to Athena as they sat by their fires and worked at making bows and arrows. It was only a dream they held, yet without that dream there would be nothing before them but the vision of generation after generation living and dying on a world that could never give them more than existence.

The dream was needed. But it, alone, was not enough. How long, on Earth, had it been from the Neolithic age to advanced civilization—how long from the time men were ready to leave their caves until they were ready to go to the stars?

Twelve thousand years.

There were men and women among the Rejects who had been specialists in various fields. There were a few books that had survived the trampling of the unicorns and others could be written with ink made from the black lance tree bark upon parchment made from the thin inner skin of unicorn hides.

The knowledge contained in the books and the learning of the Rejects still living should be preserved for the future generations. With the help of that learning perhaps they really could, someday, somehow, escape from their prison and make Athena their own.

He told West of what he had been thinking. "We'll have to start a school," he said. "This winter—tomorrow."

West nodded in agreement. "And the writings should be commenced as soon as possible. Some of the textbooks will require more time to write than Ragnarok will give the authors."

A school for the children was started the next day and the writing of the books began. The parchment books would serve two purposes. One would be to teach the future generations things that would not only help them survive but would help them create a culture of their own as advanced as the harsh environment and scanty resources of Ragnarok permitted. The other would be to warn them of the danger of a return of the Germs and to teach them all that was known about Germs and their weapons.

Lake's main contribution would be a lengthy book: TERRAN SPACESHIPS; TYPES AND OPERATION. He postponed its writing, however, to first produce a much smaller book but one that might well be more important: INTERIOR FEATURES OF A GERN CRUISER. Terran Intelligence knew a little about Gern cruisers and as second-in-command of the Constellation he had seen and studied a copy of that report. He had an excellent memory for such things, almost photographic, and he wrote the text and drew a multitude of sketches.

He shook his head ruefully at the result. The text was good but, for clarity, the accompanying illustrations should be accurate and in perspective. And he was definitely not an artist.

He discovered that Craig could take a pen in his scarred, powerful hand and draw with the neat precision of a professional artist. He turned the sketches over to him, together with the mass of specifications. Since it might someday be of such vital importance, he would make four copies of it. The text was given to a teen-age girl, who would make three more copies of it....

Four days later Schroeder handed Lake a text with some rough sketches. The title was: OPERATION OF GERN BLASTERS.

Not even Intelligence had ever been able to examine a Gern hand blaster. But a man named Schrader, on Venus, had killed a Gern with his own blaster and then disappeared with both infuriated Gerns and Gern-intimidated Venusian police in pursuit. There had been a high reward for his capture....

He looked it over and said, "I was counting on you giving us this."

Only the barest trace of surprise showed on Schroeder's face but his eyes were intently watching Lake. "So you knew all the time who I was?"

"I knew."

"Did anyone else on the Constellation know?"

"You were recognized by one of the ship's officers. You would have been tried in two more days."

"I see," Schroeder said. "And since I was guilty and couldn't be

58

returned to Earth or Venus I'd have been executed on the Constellation." He smiled sardonically. "And you, as second-in-command, would have been my execution's master of ceremonies."

Lake put the parchment sheets back together in their proper order. "Sometimes," he said, "a ship's officer has to do things that are contrary to all his own wishes."

Schroeder drew a deep breath, his face sombre with the memories he had kept to himself.

"It was two years ago when the Gerns were still talking friendship to the Earth government while they shoved the colonists around on Venus. This Gern ... there was a girl there and he thought he could do what he wanted to her because he was a mighty Gern and she was nothing. He did. That's why I killed him. I had to kill two Venusian police to get away—that's where I put the rope around my neck."

"It's not what we did but what we do that we'll live or die by on Ragnarok," Lake said. He handed Schroeder the sheets of parchment. "Tell Craig to make at least four copies of this. Someday our knowledge of Gern blasters may be something else we'll live or die by."

The school and writing were interrupted by the spring hunting. Craig made his journey to the Plateau's snow-capped mountain but he was unable to keep his promise to prospect it. The plateau was perhaps ten thousand feet in elevation and the mountain rose another ten thousand feet above the plateau. No human could climb such a mountain in a 1.5 gravity.

"I tried," he told Lake wearily when he came back. "Damn it, I never tried harder at anything in my life. It was just too much for me. Maybe some of the young ones will be better adapted and can do it when they grow up."

Craig brought back several sheets of unusually transparent mica, each sheet a foot in diameter, and a dozen large water-clear quartz crystals.

"Float, from higher up on the mountain," he said. "The mica and crystals are in place up there if we could only reach them. Other minerals, too—I panned traces in the canyon bottoms. But no iron."

Lake examined the sheets of mica. "We could make windows for the outer caves of these," he said. "Have them double thickness with a wide air space between, for insulation. As for the quartz crystals...."

"Optical instruments," Craig said. "Binoculars, microscopes—it would take us a long time to learn how to make glass as clear and flawless as those crystals. But we have no way of cutting and grinding them."

Craig went to the east that fall and to the west the next spring. He returned from the trip to the west with a twisted knee that would never let him go prospecting again.

"It will take years to find the metals we need," he said. "The indications are that we never will but I wanted to keep on trying. Now, my damned knee has me chained to these caves...."

He reconciled himself to his lameness and confinement as best he could and finished his textbook: GEOLOGY AND MINERAL IDENTIFICATION.

He also taught a geology class during the winters. It was in the winter of the year four on Ragnarok that a nine-year-old boy entered his class; the silent, scar-faced Billy Humbolt.

He was by far the youngest of Craig's students, and the most attentive. Lake was present one day when Craig asked, curiously:

"It's not often a boy your age is so interested in mineralogy and geology, Billy. Is there something more than just interest?"

"I have to learn all about minerals," Billy said with matter-of-fact seriousness, "so that when I'm grown I can find the metals for us to make a ship."

"And then?" Craig asked.

"And then we'd go to Athena, to kill the Gerns who caused my mother to die, and my grandfather, and Julia, and all the others. And to free my father and the other slaves if they're still alive."

"I see," Craig said.

He did not smile. His face was shadowed and old as he looked at the boy and beyond him; seeing again, perhaps, the frail blonde girl and the two children that the first quick, violent months had taken from him.

"I hope you succeed," he said. "I wish I was young so I could dream of the same thing. But I'm not ... so let's get back to the identification of the ores that will be needed to make a ship to go to Athena and to make blasters to kill Gerns after you get there."

Lake had a corral built early the following spring, with camouflaged wings, to trap some of the woods goats when they came. It would be an immense forward step toward conquering their new environment if they could domesticate the goats and have goat herds near the caves all through the year. Gathering enough grass to last a herd of goats through the winter would be a problem—but first, before they worried about that, they would have to see if the goats could survive the summer and winter extremes of heat and cold.

They trapped ten goats that spring. They built them brush sunshades—before summer was over the winds would have stripped the trees of most of their dry, brown leaves—and a stream of water was diverted through the corral.

It was all work in vain. The goats died from the heat in early summer, together with the young that had been born.

When fall came they trapped six more goats. They built them shelters that would be as warm as possible and carried them a large supply of the tall grass from along the creek banks; enough to last them through the winter. But the cold was too much for the goats and the second blizzard killed them all.

The next spring and fall, and with much more difficulty, they tried the experiment with pairs of unicorns. The results were the same.

Which meant they would remain a race of hunters. Ragnarok would not permit them to be herdsmen.

The years went by, each much like the one before it but for the rapid aging of the Old Ones, as Lake and the others called themselves, and the growing up of the Young Ones. No woman among the Old Ones could any longer have children, but six more normal, healthy children had been born. Like the first two, they were not affected by the gravity as Earth-born babies had been.

Among the Young Ones, Lake saw, was a distinguishable difference. Those who had been very young the day the Gerns left them to die had adapted better than those who had been a few years older.

The environment of Ragnarok had struck at the very young with merciless savagery. It had subjected them to a test of survival that was without precedent on Earth. It had killed them by the hundreds but among them had been those whose young flesh and blood and organs had resisted death by adapting to the greatest extent possible.

The day of the Old Ones was almost done and the future would soon be in the hands of the Young Ones. They were the ninety unconquerables out of what had been four thousand Rejects; the first generation of what would be a new race.

It seemed to Lake that the years came and went ever faster as the Old Ones dwindled in numbers at an accelerating rate. Anders had died in the sixth year, his heart failing him one night as he worked patiently in his crude little laboratory at carrying on the work started by Chiara to find a cure for the Hell Fever. Barber, trying to develop a strain of herbs that would grow in the lower elevation of the caves, was killed by a unicorn as he worked in his test plot below the caves. Craig went limping out one spring day on the eighth year to look at a new mineral a hunter had found a mile from the caves. A sudden cold rain blew up, chilling him before he could return, and he died of Hell Fever the same day.

Schroeder was killed by prowlers the same year, dying with his back to a tree and a bloody knife in his hand. It was the way he would have wanted to go—once he had said to Lake:

"When my times comes I would rather it be against the prowlers. They fight hard and kill quick and then they're through with you. They don't tear you up after you're dead and slobber and gloat over the pieces, the way the unicorns do."

The springs came a little earlier each year, the falls a little later, and the observations showed the suns progressing steadily northward. But the winters, though shorter, were seemingly as cold as ever. The long summers reached such a degree of heat on the ninth year that Lake knew they could endure no more than two or three years more of the increasing heat.

Then, in the summer of the tenth year, the tilting of Ragnarok—the apparent northward progress of the suns—stopped. They were in the middle of what Craig had called Big Summer and they could endure it—just barely. They would not have to leave the caves.

The suns started their drift southward. The observations were continued and carefully recorded. Big Fall was coming and behind it would be Big Winter.

Big Winter ... the threat of it worried Lake. How far to the south would the suns go—how long would they stay? Would the time come when the plateau would be buried under hundreds of feet of snow and the caves enclosed in glacial ice?

There was no way he could ever know or even guess. Only those of the future would ever know.

On the twelfth year only Lake and West were left of the Old Ones. By then there were eighty-three left of the Young Ones, eight Ragnarok-born children of the Old Ones and four Ragnarok-born children of the Young Ones. Not counting himself and West, there were ninety-five of them.

It was not many to be the beginnings of a race that would face an ice age of unknown proportions and have over them, always, the threat of a chance return of the Gerns.

The winter of the fifteenth year came and he was truly alone, the last of the Old Ones. White-haired and aged far beyond his years, he was still leader. But that winter he could do little other than sit by his fire and feel the gravity dragging at his heart. He knew, long before spring, that it was time he chose his successor.

He had hoped to live to see his son take his place—but Jim was only thirteen. Among the others was one he had been watching since the day he told Craig he would find metals to build a ship and kill the Gerns: Bill Humbolt.

63

Bill Humbolt was not the oldest among those who would make leaders but he was the most versatile of them all, the most thoughtful and stubbornly determined. He reminded Lake of that fierce old man who had been his grandfather and had it not been for the scars that twisted his face into grim ugliness he would have looked much like him.

A violent storm was roaring outside the caves the night he told the others that he wanted Bill Humbolt to be his successor. There were no objections and, without ceremony and with few words, he terminated his fifteen years of leadership.

He left the others, his son among them, and went back to the cave where he slept. His fire was low, down to dying embers, but he was too tired to build it up again. He lay down on his pallet and saw, with neither surprise nor fear, that his time was much nearer than he had thought. It was already at hand.

He lay back and let the lassitude enclose him, not fighting it. He had done the best he could for the others and now the weary journey was over.

His thoughts dissolved into the memory of the day fifteen years before. The roaring of the storm became the thunder of the Gern cruisers as they disappeared into the gray sky. Four thousand Rejects stood in the cold wind and watched them go, the children not yet understanding that they had been condemned to die. Somehow, his own son was among them——

He tried feebly to rise. There was work to do—a lot of work to do....

PART 2

It was early morning as Bill Humbolt sat by the fire in his cave and studied the map Craig had made of the plateau's mountain. Craig had left the mountain nameless and he dipped his pen in ink to write: Craig Mountains.

"Bill——"

Delmont Anders entered very quietly, what he had to tell already evident on his face.

"He died last night, Bill."

It was something he had been expecting to come at any time but the lack of surprise did not diminish the sense of loss. Lake had been the last of the Old Ones, the last of those who had worked and fought and shortened the years of their lives that the Young Ones might have a chance to live. Now he was gone—now a brief era was ended, a valiant, bloody chapter written and finished.

And he was the new leader who would decree how the next chapter should be written, only four years older than the boy who was looking at him with an unconscious appeal for reassurance on his face....

"You'd better tell Jim," he said. "Then, a little later, I want to talk to everyone about the things we'll start doing as soon as spring comes."

"You mean, the hunting?" Delmont asked.

"No—more than just the hunting."

He sat for a while after Delmont left, looking back down the years that had preceded that day, back to that first morning on Ragnarok.

He had set a goal for himself that morning when he left his toy bear in the dust behind him and walked beside Julia into the new and

65

perilous way of life. He had promised himself that some day he would watch the Gerns die and beg for mercy as they died and he would give them the same mercy they had given his mother.

As he grew older he realized that his hatred, alone, was a futile thing. There would have to be a way of leaving Ragnarok and there would have to be weapons with which to fight the Gerns. These would be things impossible and beyond his reach unless he had the help of all the others in united, coordinated effort.

To make certain of that united effort he would have to be their leader. So for eleven years he had studied and trained until there was no one who could use a bow or spear quite as well as he could, no one who could travel as far in a day or spot a unicorn ambush as quickly. And there was no one, with the exception of George Ord, who had studied as many textbooks as he had.

He had reached his first goal—he was leader. For all of them there existed the second goal: the hope of someday leaving Ragnarok and taking Athena from the Gerns. For many of them, perhaps, it was only wishful dreaming but for him it was the prime driving force of his life.

There was so much for them to do and their lives were so short in which to do it. For so long as he was leader they would not waste a day in idle wishing....

When the others were gathered to hear what he had to say he spoke to them:

"We're going to continue where the Old Ones had to leave off. We're better adapted than they were and we're going to find metals to make a ship if there are any to be found.

"Somewhere on Ragnarok, on the northwest side of a range similar to the Craig Mountains on the plateau, is a deep valley that the Dunbar Expedition called the Chasm. They didn't investigate it closely since their instruments showed no metals there but they saw strata in one place that was red; an iron discoloration. Maybe we can find a vein there that was too small for them to have paid any attention to. So we'll go over the Craigs as soon as the snow melts from them."

"That will be in early summer," George Ord said, his black eyes

66

thoughtful. "Whoever goes will have to time their return for either just before the prowlers and unicorns come back from the north or wait until they've all migrated down off the plateau."

It was something Humbolt had been thinking about and wishing they could remedy. Men could elude unicorn attacks wherever there were trees large enough to offer safety and even prowler attacks could be warded off wherever there were trees for refuge; spears holding back the prowlers who would climb the trees while arrows picked off the ones on the ground. But there were no trees on the plateau, and to be caught by a band of prowlers or unicorns there was certain death for any small party of two or three. For that reason no small parties had ever gone up on the plateau except when the unicorns and prowlers were gone or nearly so. It was an inconvenience and it would continue for as long as their weapons were the slow-to-reload bows.

"You're supposed to be our combination inventor-craftsman," he said to George. "No one else can compare with you in that respect. Besides, you're not exactly enthusiastic about such hard work as mountain climbing. So from now on you'll do the kind of work you're best fitted for. Your first job is to make us a better bow. Make it like a crossbow, with a sliding action to draw and cock the string and with a magazine of arrows mounted on top of it."

George studied the idea thoughtfully. "The general principle is simple," he said. "I'll see what I can do."

"How many of us will go over the Craig Mountains, Bill?" Dan Barber asked.

"You and I," Humbolt answered. "A three-man party under Bob Craig will go into the Western Hills and another party under Johnny Stevens will go into the Eastern Hills."

He looked toward the adjoining cave where the guns had been stored for so long, coated with unicorn tallow to protect them from rust.

"We could make gun powder if we could find a deposit of saltpeter. We already know where there's a little sulphur. The guns would have to be converted to flintlocks, though, since we don't have what we need for cartridge priming material. Worse, we'd have to use

67

ceramic bullets. They would be inefficient—too light, and destructive to the bores. But we would need powder for mining if we ever found any iron. And, if we can't have metal bullets to shoot the Gerns, we can have bombs to blast them with."

"Suppose," Johnny Stevens said, "that we never do find the metals to make a ship. How will we ever leave Ragnarok if that happens?"

"There's another way—a possible way—of leaving here without a ship of our own. If there are no metals we'll have to try it."

"Why wait?" Bob Craig demanded. "Why not try it now?"

"Because the odds would be about ten thousand to one in favor of the Gerns. But we'll try it if everything else fails."

George made, altered, and rejected four different types of crossbows before he perfected a reloading bow that met his critical approval. He brought it to where Humbolt stood outside the caves early one spring day when the grass was sending up the first green shoots on the southern hillsides and the long winter was finally dying.

"Here it is," he said, handing Humbolt the bow. "Try it."

He took it, noting the fine balance of it. Projecting down from the center of the bow, at right angles to it, was a stock shaped to fit the grip of the left hand. Under the crossbar was a sliding stock for the right hand, shaped like the butt of a pistol and fitted with a trigger. Mounted slightly above and to one side of the crossbar was a magazine containing ten short arrows.

The pistol grip was in position near the forestock. He pulled it back the length of the crossbar and it brought the string with it, stretching it taut. There was a click as the trigger mechanism locked the bowstring in place and at the same time a concealed spring arrangement shoved an arrow into place against the string.

He took quick aim at a distant tree and pressed the trigger. There was a twang as the arrow was ejected. He jerked the sliding pistol grip forward and back to reload, pressing the trigger an instant later. Another arrow went its way.

By the time he had fired the tenth arrow in the magazine he was

68

shooting at the rate of one arrow per second. On the trunk of the distant tree, like a bristle of stiff whiskers, the ten arrows were driven deep into the wood in an area no larger than the chest of a prowler or head of a unicorn.

"This is better than I hoped for," he said to George. "One man with one of these would equal six men with ordinary bows."

"I'm going to add another feature," George said. "Bundles of arrows, ten to the bundle in special holders, to carry in the quivers. To reload the magazine you'd just slap down a new bundle of arrows, in no more time than it would take to put one arrow in an ordinary bow. I figured that with practice a man should be able to get off forty arrows in not much more than twenty seconds."

George took the bow and went back in the cave to add his new feature. Humbolt stared after him, thinking, If he can make something like that out of wood and unicorn gut, what would he be able to give us if he could have metal?

Perhaps George would never have the opportunity to show what he could do with metal. But Humbolt already felt sure that George's genius would, if it ever became necessary, make possible the alternate plan for leaving Ragnarok.

The weeks dragged into months and at last enough snow was gone from the Craigs that Humbolt and Dan Barber could start. They met no opposition. The prowlers had long since disappeared into the north and the unicorns were very scarce. They had no occasion to test the effectiveness of the new automatic crossbows in combat; a lack of opportunity that irked Barber.

"Any other time, if we had ordinary bows," he complained, "the unicorns would be popping up to charge us from all directions."

"Don't fret," Humbolt consoled him. "This fall, when we come back, they will be."

They reached the mountain and stopped near its foot where a creek came down, its water high and muddy with melting snows. There they hunted until they had obtained all the meat they could carry. They would see no more game when they went up the mountain's canyons. A poisonous weed replaced most of the grass in all the canyons and the animals of Ragnarok had learned long before to shun the mountain.

They found the canyon that Craig and his men had tried to explore and started up it. It was there that Craig had discovered the quartz and mica and so far as he had been able to tell the head of that canyon would be the lowest of all the passes over the mountain.

The canyon went up the mountain diagonally so that the climb was not steep although it was constant. They began to see mica and quartz crystals in the creek bed and at noon on the second day they passed the last stunted tree. Nothing grew higher than that point but the thorny poison weeds and they were scarce.

The air was noticeably thinner there and their burdens heavier. A short distance beyond they came to a small rock monument; Craig's turn-back point.

The next day they found the quartz crystals in place. A mile farther was the vein the mica had come from. Of the other minerals Craig had hoped to find, however, there were only traces.

The fourth day was an eternity of struggling up the now-steeper canyon under loads that seemed to weigh hundreds of pounds; forcing their protesting legs to carry them fifty steps at a time, at the end of which they would stop to rest while their lungs labored to suck in the thin air in quick, panting breaths.

It would have been much easier to have gone around the mountain. But the Chasm was supposed to be like a huge cavity scooped out of the plateau beyond the mountain, rimmed with sheer cliffs a mile high. Only on the side next to the mountain was there a slope leading down into it.

They stopped for the night where the creek ended in a small spring. There the snow still clung to the canyon's walls and there the canyon curved, offering them the promise of the summit just around the bend as it had been doing all day.

The sun was hot and bright the next morning as they made their slow way on again. The canyon straightened, the steep walls of it flattening out to make a pair of ragged shoulders with a saddle between them.

They climbed to the summit of the saddle and there, suddenly before them, was the other side of the world—and the Chasm.

Far below them was a plateau, stretching endlessly like the one they had left behind them. But the chasm dominated all else. It was a gigantic, sheer-walled valley, a hundred miles long by forty miles wide, sunk deep in the plateau with the tops of its mile-high walls level with the floor of the plateau. The mountain under them dropped swiftly away, sloping down and down to the level of the plateau and then on, down and down again, to the bottom of the chasm that was so deep its floor was half hidden by the morning shadows.

"My God!" Barber said. "It must be over three miles under us to the bottom, on the vertical. Ten miles of thirty-three per cent grade—if we go down we'll never get out again."

"You can turn back here if you want to," Humbolt said.

"Turn back?" Barber's red whiskers seemed to bristle. "Who in hell said anything about turning back?"

"Nobody," Humbolt said, smiling a little at Barber's quick flash of anger.

He studied the chasm, wishing that they could have some way of cutting the quartz crystals and making binoculars. It was a long way to look with the naked eye....

Here and there the chasm thrust out arms into the plateau. All the arms were short, however, and even at their heads the cliffs were vertical. The morning shadows prevented a clear view of much of the chasm and he could see no sign of the red-stained strata that they were searching for.

In the southwest corner of the chasm, far away and almost imperceptible, he saw a faint cloud rising up from the chasm's floor. It was impossible to tell what it was and it faded away as he watched.

Barber saw it, too, and said, "It looked like smoke. Do you suppose there could be people—or some kind of intelligent things—living down there?"

"It might have been the vapor from hot springs, condensed by the

71

cool morning air," he said. "Whatever it was, we'll look into it when we get there."

The climb down the steep slope into the chasm was swifter than that up the canyon but no more pleasant. Carrying a heavy pack down such a grade exerted a torturous strain upon the backs of the legs.

The heat increased steadily as they descended. They reached the floor of the valley the next day and the noonday heat was so great that Humbolt wondered if they might not have trapped themselves into what the summer would soon transform into a monstrous oven where no life at all could exist. There could never be any choice, of course—the mountains were passable only when the weather was hot.

The floor of the valley was silt, sand and gravel—they would find nothing there. They set out on a circuit of the chasm's walls, following along close to the base.

In many places the mile-high walls were without a single ledge to break their vertical faces. When they came to the first such place they saw that the ground near the base was riddled with queer little pits, like tiny craters of the moon. As they looked there was a crack like a cannon shot and the ground beside them erupted into an explosion of sand and gravel. When the dust had cleared away there was a new crater where none had been before.

Humbolt wiped the blood from his face where a flying fragment had cut it and said, "The heat of the sun loosens rocks up on the rim. When one falls a mile in a one point five gravity, it's traveling like a meteor."

They went on, through the danger zone. As with the peril of the chasm's heat, there was no choice. Only by observing the material that littered the base of the cliffs could they know what minerals, if any, might be above them.

On the fifteenth day they saw the red-stained stratum. Humbolt quickened his pace, hurrying forward in advance of Barber. The stratum was too high up on the wall to be reached but it was not necessary to examine it in place—the base of the cliff was piled thick with fragments from it.

He felt the first touch of discouragement as he looked at them. They

72

were a sandstone, light in weight. The iron present was only what the Dunbar Expedition had thought it to be; a mere discoloration.

They made their way slowly along the foot of the cliff, examining piece after piece in the hope of finding something more than iron stains. There was no variation, however, and a mile farther on they came to the end of the red stratum. Beyond that point the rocks were gray, without a vestige of iron.

"So that," Barber said, looking back the way they had come, "is what we were going to build a ship out of—iron stains!"

Humbolt did not answer. For him it was more than a disappointment. It was the death of a dream he had held since the year he was nine and had heard that the Dunbar Expedition had seen iron-stained rock in a deep chasm—the only iron-stained rock on the face of Ragnarok. Surely, he had thought, there would be enough iron there to build a small ship. For eleven years he had worked toward the day when he would find it. Now, he had found it—and it was nothing. The ship was as far away as ever....

But discouragement was as useless as iron-stained sandstone. He shook it off and turned to Barber.

"Let's go," he said. "Maybe we'll find something by the time we circle the chasm."

For seven days they risked the danger of death from downward plunging rocks and found nothing. On the eighth day they found the treasure that was not treasure.

They stopped for the evening just within the mouth of one of the chasm's tributaries. Humbolt went out to get a drink where a trickle of water ran through the sand and as he knelt down he saw the flash of something red under him, almost buried in the sand.

He lifted it out. It was a stone half the size of his hand; darkly translucent and glowing in the light of the setting sun like blood.

It was a ruby.

He looked, and saw another gleam a little farther up the stream. It was another ruby, almost as large as the first one. Near it was a

73

flawless blue sapphire. Scattered here and there were smaller rubies and sapphires, down to the size of grains of sand.

He went farther upstream and saw specimens of still another stone. They were colorless but burning with internal fires. He rubbed one of them hard across the ruby he still carried and there was a gritting sound as it cut a deep scratch in the ruby.

"I'll be damned," he said aloud.

There was only one stone hard enough to cut a ruby—the diamond.

It was almost dark when he returned to where Barber was resting beside their packs.

"What did you find to keep you out so late?" Barber asked curiously.

He dropped a double handful of rubies, sapphires and diamonds at Barber's feet.

"Take a look," he said. "On a civilized world what you see there would buy us a ship without our having to lift a finger. Here they're just pretty rocks.

"Except the diamonds," he added "At least we now have something to cut those quartz crystals with."

They took only a few of the rubies and sapphires the next morning but they gathered more of the diamonds, looking in particular for the gray-black and ugly but very hard and tough carbonado variety. Then they resumed their circling of the chasm's walls.

The heat continued its steady increase as the days went by. Only at night was there any relief from it and the nights were growing swiftly shorter as the blue sun rose earlier each morning. When the yellow sun rose the chasm became a blazing furnace around the edge of which they crept like ants in some gigantic oven.

There was no life in any form to be seen; no animal or bush or blade of grass. There was only the barren floor of the chasm, made a harsh green shade by the two suns and writhing and undulating with heat

74

waves like a nightmare sea, while above them the towering cliffs shimmered, too, and sometimes seemed to be leaning far out over their heads and already falling down upon them.

They found no more minerals of any kind and they came at last to the place where they had seen the smoke or vapor.

There the walls of the chasm drew back to form a little valley a mile long by half a mile wide. The walls did not drop vertically to the floor there but sloped out at the base into a fantastic formation of natural roofs and arches that reached almost to the center of the valley from each side. Green things grew in the shade under the arches and sparkling waterfalls cascaded down over many of them. A small creek carried the water out of the valley, going out into the chasm a little way before the hot sands absorbed it.

They stood and watched for some time, but there was no movement in the valley other than the waving of the green plants as a breeze stirred them. Once the breeze shifted to bring them the fresh, sweet scent of growing things and urge them to come closer.

"A place like that doesn't belong here," Barber said in a low voice. "But it's there. I wonder what else is there?"

"Shade and cool water," Humbolt said. "And maybe things that don't like strangers. Let's go find out."

They watched warily as they walked, their crossbows in their hands. At the closer range they saw that the roofs and arches were the outer remains of a system of natural caves that went back into the valley's walls. The green vegetation grew wherever the roofs gave part-time shade, consisting mainly of a holly-leafed bush with purple flowers and a tall plant resembling corn.

Under some of the roofs the corn was mature, the orange colored grains visible. Under others it was no more than half grown. He saw the reason and said to Barber:

"There are both warm and cold springs here. The plants watered by the warm springs would grow almost the year around; the ones watered by the cold springs only in the summer. And what we saw from the mountain top would have been vapor rising from the warm springs."

75

They passed under arch after arch without seeing any life. When they came to the valley's upper end and still had seen nothing it seemed evident that there was little danger of an encounter with any intelligent-and-hostile creatures. Apparently nothing at all lived in the little valley.

Humbolt stopped under a broad arch where the breeze was made cool and moist by the spray of water it had come through. Barber went on, to look under the adjoining arch.

Caves led into the wall from both arches and as he stood there Humbolt saw something lying in the mouth of the nearest cave. It was a little mound of orange corn; lying in a neat pile as though whatever had left it there had intended to come back after it.

He looked toward the other arch but Barber was somewhere out of sight. He doubted that whatever had left the corn could be much of a menace—dangerous animals were more apt to eat flesh than corn—but he went to the cave with his crossbow ready.

He stopped at the mouth of the cave to let his eyes become accustomed to the darkness inside it. As he did so the things inside came out to meet him.

They emerged into full view; six little animals the size of squirrels, each of them a different color. They walked on short hind legs like miniature bears and the dark eyes in the bear-chipmunk faces were fixed on him with intense interest. They stopped five feet in front of him, there to stand in a neat row and continue the fascinated staring up at him.

The yellow one in the center scratched absently at its stomach with a furry paw and he lowered the bow, feeling a little foolish at having bothered to raise it against animals so small and harmless.

Then he half brought it up again as the yellow one opened its mouth and said in a tone that held distinct anticipation:

"I think we'll eat you for supper."

He darted glances to right and left but there was nothing near him except the six little animals. The yellow one, having spoken, was staring silently at him with only curiosity on its furry face. He

76

wondered if some miasma or some scent from the vegetation in the valley had warped his mind into sudden insanity and asked:

"You think you'll do what?"

It opened its mouth again, to stutter, "I—I——" Then, with a note of alarm, "Hey...."

It said no more and the next sound was that of Barber hurrying toward him and calling, "Hey—Bill—where are you?"

"Here," he answered, and he was already sure that he knew why the little animal had spoken to him.

Barber came up and saw the six chipmunk-bears. "Six of them!" he exclaimed. "There's one in the next cave—the damned thing spoke to me!"

"I thought so," he replied. "You told it we'd have it for supper and then it said, 'You think you'll do what?' didn't it?"

Barber's face showed surprise. "How did you know that?"

"They're telepathic between one another," he said. "The yellow one there repeated what the one you spoke to heard you say and it repeated what the yellow one heard me say. It has to be telepathy between them."

"Telepathy——" Barber stared at the six little animals, who stared back with their fascinated curiosity undiminished. "But why should they want to repeat aloud what they receive telepathically?"

"I don't know. Maybe at some stage in their evolution only part of them were telepaths and the telepaths broadcasted danger warnings to the others that way. So far as that goes, why does a parrot repeat what it hears?"

There was a scurry of movement behind Barber and another of the little animals, a white one, hurried past them. It went to the yellow one and they stood close together as they stared up. Apparently they were mates....

"That's the other one—those are the two that mocked us," Barber

77

said, and thereby gave them the name by which they would be known: mockers.

The mockers were fresh meat—but they accepted the humans with such friendliness and trust that Barber lost all his desire to have one for supper or for any other time. They had a limited supply of dried meat and there would be plenty of orange corn. They would not go hungry.

They discovered that the mockers had living quarters in both the cool caves and the ones warmed by the hot springs. There was evidence that they hibernated during the winters in the warm caves.

There were no minerals in the mockers' valley and they set out to continue their circuit of the chasm. They did not get far until the heat had become so great that the chasm's tributaries began going dry. They turned back then, to wait in the little valley until the fall rains came.

When the long summer was ended by the first rain they resumed their journey. They took a supply of the orange corn and two of the mockers; the yellow one and its mate. The other mockers watched them leave, standing silent and solemn in front of their caves as though they feared they might never see their two fellows or the humans again.

The two mockers were pleasant company, riding on their shoulders and chattering any nonsense that came to mind. And sometimes saying things that were not at all nonsense, making Humbolt wonder if mockers could partly read human minds and dimly understand the meaning of some of the things they said.

They found a place where saltpeter was very thinly and erratically distributed. They scraped off all the films of it that were visible and procured a small amount. They completed their circuit and reached the foot of the long, steep slope of the Craigs without finding anything more.

It was an awesome climb that lay before them; up a grade so steep and barred with so many low ledges that when their legs refused to carry them farther they crawled. The heat was still very serious and there would be no water until they came to the spring beyond the mountain's summit. A burning wind, born on the blazing floor of the chasm, followed them up the mountain all day. Their leather canteens were almost dry when night came and they were no more than a third of the way to the top.

The mockers had become silent as the elevation increased and when they stopped for the night Humbolt saw that they would never live to cross the mountain. They were breathing fast, their hearts racing, as they tried to extract enough oxygen from the thin air. They drank a few drops of water but they would not touch the corn he offered them.

The white mocker died at midmorning the next day as they stopped for a rest. The yellow one crawled feebly to her side and died a few minutes later.

"So that's that," Humbolt said, looking down at them. "The only things on Ragnarok that ever trusted us and wanted to be our friends—and we killed them."

They drank the last of their water and went on. They made dry camp that night and dreams of cold streams of water tormented their exhausted sleep. The next day was a hellish eternity in which they walked and fell and crawled and walked and fell again.

Barber weakened steadily, his breathing growing to a rattling panting. He spoke once that afternoon, to try to smile with dry, swollen lips and say between his panting gasps, "It would be hell—to have to die—so thirsty like this."

After that he fell with increasing frequency, each time slower and weaker in getting up again. Half a mile short of the summit he fell for the last time. He tried to get up, failed, and tried to crawl. He failed at that, too, and collapsed face down in the rocky soil.

Humbolt went to him and said between his own labored intakes of breath, "Wait, Dan—I'll go on—bring you back water."

Barber raised himself with a great effort and looked up. "No use," he said. "My heart—too much——"

He fell forward again and that time he was very still, his desperate panting no more.

79

It seemed to Humbolt that it was half a lifetime later that he finally reached the spring and the cold, clear water. He drank, the most ecstatic pleasure he had ever experienced in his life. Then the pleasure drained away as he seemed to see Dan Barber trying to smile and seemed to hear him say, "It would be hell—to have to die—so thirsty like this."

He rested for two days before he was in condition to continue on his way. He reached the plateau and saw that the woods goats had been migrating south for some time. On the second morning he climbed up a gentle roll in the plain and met three unicorns face to face.

They charged at once, squealing with anticipation. Had he been equipped with an ordinary bow he would have been killed within seconds. But the automatic crossbow poured a rain of arrows into the faces of the unicorns that caused them to swing aside in pain and enraged astonishment. The moment they had swung enough to expose the area just behind their heads the arrows became fatal.

One unicorn escaped, three arrows bristling in its face. It watched him from a distance for a little while, squealing and shaking its head in baffled fury. Then it turned and disappeared over a swell in the plain, running like a deer.

He resumed his southward march, hurrying faster than before. The unicorn had headed north and that could be for but one purpose: to bring enough reinforcements to finish the job.

He reached the caves at night. No one was up but George Ord, working late in his combination workshop-laboratory.

George looked up at the sound of his entrance and saw that he was alone. "So Dan didn't make it?" he asked.

"The chasm got him," he answered. And then, wearily, "The chasm—we found the damned thing."

"The red stratum——"

"It was only iron stains."

"I made a little pilot smelter while you were gone," George said. "I was hoping the red stratum would be ore. The other prospecting parties—none of them found anything."

"We'll try again next spring," he said. "We'll find it somewhere, no matter how long it takes."

"Our time may not be so long. The observations show the sun to be farther south than ever."

"Then we'll make double use of the time we do have. We'll cut the hunting parties to the limit and send out more prospecting parties. We're going to have a ship to meet the Gerns again."

"Sometimes," George said, his black eyes studying him thoughtfully, "I think that's all you live for, Bill: for the day when you can kill Gerns."

George said it as a statement of a fact, without censure, but Humbolt could not keep an edge of harshness out of his voice as he answered:

"For as long as I'm leader that's all we're all going to live for."

He followed the game south that fall, taking with him Bob Craig and young Anders. Hundreds of miles south of the caves they came to the lowlands; a land of much water and vegetation and vast herds of unicorns and woods goats. It was an exceedingly dangerous country, due to the concentration of unicorns and prowlers, and only the automatic crossbows combined with never ceasing vigilance enabled them to survive.

There they saw the crawlers; hideous things that crawled on multiple legs like three-ton centipedes, their mouths set with six mandibles and dripping a stinking saliva. The bite of a crawler was poisonous, instantly paralyzing even to a unicorn, though not instantly killing them. The crawlers ate their victims at once, however, ripping the helpless and still living flesh from its bones.

Although the unicorns feared the crawlers, the prowlers hated them with a fanatical intensity and made use of their superior quickness to kill every crawler they found; ripping at the crawler until the crawler, in an insanity of rage, bit itself and died of its own poison.

They had taken one of the powerful longbows with them, in addition

81

to their crossbows, and they killed a crawler with it one day. As they did so a band of twenty prowlers came suddenly upon them.

Twenty prowlers, with the advantage of surprise at short range, could have slaughtered them. Instead, the prowlers continued on their way without as much as a challenging snarl.

"Now why," Bob Craig wondered, "did they do that?"

"They saw we had just killed a crawler," Humbolt said. "The crawlers are their enemies and I guess letting us live was their way of showing appreciation."

Their further explorations of the lowlands revealed no minerals—nothing but alluvial material of unknown depth—and there was no reason to stay longer except that return to the caves was impossible until spring came. They built attack-proof shelters in the trees and settled down to wait out the winter.

They started north with the first wave of woods goats, nothing but lack of success to show for their months of time and effort.

When they were almost to the caves they came to the barren valley where the Gerns had herded the Rejects out of the cruisers and to the place where the stockade had been. It was a lonely place, the stockade walls fallen and scattered and the graves of Humbolt's mother and all the others long since obliterated by the hooves of the unicorn legions. Bitter memories were reawakened, tinged by the years with nostalgia, and the stockade was far behind them before the dark mood left him.

The orange corn was planted that spring and the number of prospecting parties was doubled.

The corn sprouted, grew feebly, and died before maturity. The prospecting parties returned one by one, each to report no success. He decided, that fall, that time was too precious to waste—they would have to use the alternate plan he had spoken of.

He went to George Ord and asked him if it would be possible to build a hyperspace transmitter with the materials they had.

"It's the one way we could have a chance to leave here without a ship of our own," he said. "By luring a Gern cruiser here and then taking it away from them."

George shook his head. "A hyperspace transmitter might be built, given enough years of time. But it would be useless without power. It would take a generator of such size that we'd have to melt down every gun, knife, axe, every piece of steel and iron we have. And then we'd be five hundred pounds short. On top of that, we'd have to have at least three hundred pounds more of copper for additional wire."

"I didn't realize it would take such a large generator," he said after a silence. "I was sure we could have a transmitter."

"Get me the metal and we can," George said. He sighed restlessly and there was almost hatred in his eyes as he looked at the inclosing walls of the cave. "You're not the only one who would like to leave our prison. Get me eight hundred pounds of copper and iron and I'll make the transmitter, some way."

Eight hundred pounds of metal.... On Ragnarok that was like asking for the sun.

The years went by and each year there was the same determined effort, the same lack of success. And each year the suns were farther south, marking the coming of the end of any efforts other than the one to survive.

In the year thirty, when fall came earlier than ever before, he was forced to admit to himself the bleak and bitter fact: he and the others were not of the generation that would escape from Ragnarok. They were Earth-born—they were not adapted to Ragnarok and could not scour a world of 1.5 gravity for metals that might not exist.

And vengeance was a luxury he could not have.

A question grew in his mind where there had been only his hatred for the Gerns before. What would become of the future generations on Ragnarok?

With the question a scene from his childhood kept coming back to him; a late summer evening in the first year on Ragnarok and Julia sitting beside him in the warm starlight....

"You're my son, Billy," she had said. "The first I ever had. Now, before so very long, maybe I'll have another one."

Hesitantly, not wanting to believe, he had asked, "What some of them said about how you might die then—it won't really happen, will it, Julia?"

"It ... might." Then her arm had gone around him and she had said, "If I do I'll leave in my place a life that's more important than mine ever was.

"Remember me, Billy, and this evening, and what I said to you, if you should ever be leader. Remember that it's only through the children that we can ever survive and whip this world. Protect them while they're small and helpless and teach them to fight and be afraid of nothing when they're a little older. Never, never let them forget how they came to be on Ragnarok. Someday, even if it's a hundred years from now, the Gerns will come again and they must be ready to fight, for their freedom and for their lives."

He had been too young then to understand how truly she had spoken and when he was old enough his hatred for the Gerns had blinded him to everything but his own desires. Now, he could see....

The children of each generation would be better adapted to Ragnarok and full adaptation would eventually come. But all the generations of the future would be potential slaves of the Gern Empire, free only so long as they remained unnoticed.

It was inconceivable that the Gerns should never pass by Ragnarok through all time to come. And when they finally came the slow, uneventful progression of decades and centuries might have brought a false sense of security to the people of Ragnarok, might have turned the stories of what the Gerns did to the Rejects into legends and then into myths that no one any longer believed.

The Gerns would have to be brought to Ragnarok before that could happen.

He went to George Ord again and said:

"There's one kind of transmitter we could make a generator for—a plain normal-space transmitter, dot-dash, without a receiver."

84

George laid down the diamond cutting wheel he had been working on.

"It would take two hundred years for the signal to get to Athena at the speed of light," he said. "Then, forty days after it got there, a Gern cruiser would come hell-bent to investigate."

"I want the ones of the future to know that the Gerns will be here no later than two hundred years from now. And with always the chance that a Gern cruiser in space might pick up the signal at any time before then."

"I see," George said. "The sword of Damocles hanging over their heads, to make them remember."

"You know what would happen to them if they ever forgot. You're as old as I am—you know what the Gerns did to us."

"I'm older than you are," George said. "I was nine when the Gerns left us here. They kept my father and mother and my sister was only three. I tried to keep her warm by holding her but the Hell Fever got her that first night. She was too young to understand why I couldn't help her more...."

Hatred burned in his eyes at the memory, like some fire that had been banked but had never died. "Yes, I remember the Gerns and what they did. I wouldn't want it to have to happen to others—the transmitter will be made so that it won't."

The guns were melted down, together with other items of iron and steel, to make the castings for the generator. Ceramic pipes were made to carry water from the spring to a waterwheel. The long, slow job of converting the miscellany of electronic devices, many of them broken, into the components of a transmitter proceeded.

It was five years before the transmitter was ready for testing. It was early fall of the year thirty-five then, and the water that gushed from the pipe splashed in cold drops against Humbolt as the waterwheel was set in motion.

The generator began to hum and George observed the output of it and the transmitter as registered by the various meters he had made.

"Weak, but it will reach the Gern monitor station on Athena," he said, "It's ready to send—what do you want to say?"

"Make it something short," he said. "Make it, 'Ragnarok calling.'"

George poised his finger over the transmitting key. "This will set forces in motion that can never be recalled. What we do here this morning is going to cause a lot of Gerns—or Ragnarok people—to die."

"It will be the Gerns who die," he said. "Send the signal."

"Like you, I believe the same thing," George said. "I have to believe it because that's the way I want it to be. I hope we're right. It's something we'll never know."

He began depressing the key.

A boy was given the job of operating the key and the signal went out daily until the freezing of winter stopped the waterwheel that powered the generator.

The sending of the signals was resumed when spring came and the prospecting parties continued their vain search for metals.

The suns continued moving south and each year the springs came later, the falls earlier. In the spring of forty-five he saw that he would have to make his final decision.

By then they had dwindled until they numbered only sixty-eight; the Young Ones gray and rapidly growing old. There was no longer any use to continue the prospecting—if any metals were to be found they were at the north end of the plateau where the snow no longer melted during the summer. They were too few to do more than prepare for what the Old Ones had feared they might have to face— Big Winter. That would require the work of all of them.

Sheets of mica were brought down from the Craigs, the summits of which were deeply buried under snow even in midsummer. Stoves were made of fireclay and mica, which would give both heat and light and would be more efficient than the open fireplaces. The innermost caves were prepared for occupation, with multiple doors

86

to hold out the cold and with laboriously excavated ventilation ducts and smoke outlets.

There were sixty of them in the fall of fifty, when all had been done that could be done to prepare for what might come.

"There aren't many of the Earth-born left now," Bob Craig said to him one night as they sat in the flickering light of a stove. "And there hasn't been time for there to be many of the Ragnarok-born. The Gerns wouldn't get many slaves if they should come now."

"They could use however many they found," he answered. "The younger ones, who are the best adapted to this gravity, would be exceptionally strong and quick on a one-gravity world. There are dangerous jobs where a strong, quick slave is a lot more efficient and expendable than complex, expensive machines."

"And they would want some specimens for scientific study," Jim Lake said. "They would want to cut into the young ones and see how they're built that they're adapted to this one and a half gravity world."

He smiled with the cold mirthlessness that always reminded Humbolt of his father—of the Lake who had been the Constellation's lieutenant commander. "According to the books the Gerns never did try to make it a secret that when a Gern doctor or biologist cuts into the muscles or organs of a non-Gern to see what makes them tick, he wants them to be still alive and ticking as he does so."

Seventeen-year-old Don Chiara spoke, to say slowly, thoughtfully:

"Slavery and vivisection.... If the Gerns should come now when there are so few of us, and if we should fight the best we could and lose, it would be better for whoever was the last of us left to put a knife in the hearts of the women and children than to let the Gerns have them."

No one made any answer. There was no answer to make, no alternative to suggest.

"In the future there will be more of us and it will be different," he said at last. "On Earth the Gerns were always stronger and faster

87

than humans but when the Gerns come to Ragnarok they're going to find a race that isn't really human any more. They're going to find a race before which they'll be like woods goats before prowlers."

"If only they don't come too soon," Craig said.

"That was the chance that had to be taken," he replied.

He wondered again as he spoke, as he had wondered so often in the past years, if he had given them all their death sentence when he ordered the transmitter built. Yet, the future generations could not be permitted to forget ... and steel could not be tempered without first thrusting it into the fire.

He was the last of the Young Ones when he awoke one night in the fall of fifty-six and found himself burning with the Hell Fever. He did not summon any of the others. They could do nothing for him and he had already done all he could for them.

He had done all he could for them ... and now he would leave forty-nine men, women and children to face the unknown forces of Big Winter while over them hung the sword he had forged; the increasing danger of detection by the Gerns.

The question came again, sharp with the knowledge that it was far too late for him to change any of it. Did I arrange the execution of my people?

Then, through the red haze of the fever, Julia spoke to him out of the past; sitting again beside him in the summer twilight and saying:

Remember me, Billy, and this evening, and what I said to you ... teach them to fight and be afraid of nothing ... never let them forget how they came to be on Ragnarok....

She seemed very near and real and the doubt faded and was gone. Teach them to fight ... never let them forget.... The men of Ragnarok were only fur-clad hunters who crouched in caves but they would grow in numbers as time went by. Each generation would be stronger than the generation before it and he had set forces in motion that would bring the last generation the trial of combat and the opportunity for freedom. How well they fought on that day would determine their destiny but he was certain, once again, what that destiny would be.

It would be to walk as conquerors before beaten and humbled Gerns.

It was winter of the year eighty-five and the temperature was one hundred and six degrees below zero. Walter Humbolt stood in front of the ice tunnel that led back through the glacier to the caves and looked up into the sky.

It was noon but there was no sun in the starlit sky. Many weeks before the sun had slipped below the southern horizon. For a little while a dim halo had marked its passage each day; then that, too, had faded away. But now it was time for the halo to appear again, to herald the sun's returning.

Frost filled the sky, making the stars flicker as it swirled endlessly downward. He blinked against it, his eyelashes trying to freeze to his lower eyelids at the movement, and turned to look at the north.

There the northern lights were a gigantic curtain that filled a third of the sky, rippling and waving in folds that pulsated in red and green, rose and lavender and violet. Their reflection gleamed on the glacier that sloped down from the caves and glowed softly on the other glacier; the one that covered the transmitter station. The transmitter had long ago been taken into the caves but the generator and waterwheel were still there, frozen in a tomb of ice.

For three years the glacier had been growing before the caves and the plateau's southern face had been buried under snow for ten years. Only a few woods goats ever came as far north as the country south of the caves and they stayed only during the brief period between the last snow of spring and the first snow of fall. Their winter home was somewhere down near the equator. What had been called the Southern Lowlands was a frozen, lifeless waste.

Once they had thought about going to the valley in the chasm where the mockers would be hibernating in their warm caves. But even if they could have gone up the plateau and performed the incredible feat of crossing the glacier-covered, blizzard-ripped Craigs, they

89

would have found no food in the mockers' valley—only a little corn the mockers had stored away, which would soon have been exhausted.

There was no place for them to live but in the caves or as nomads migrating with the animals. And if they migrated to the equator each year they would have to leave behind them all the books and tools and everything that might someday have given them a civilized way of life and might someday have shown them how to escape from their prison.

He looked again to the south where the halo should be, thinking: They should have made their decision in there by now. I'm their leader—but I can't force them to stay here against their will. I could only ask them to consider what it would mean if we left here.

Snow creaked underfoot as he moved restlessly. He saw something lying under the blanket of frost and went to it. It was an arrow that someone had dropped. He picked it up, carefully, because the intense cold had made the shaft as brittle as glass. It would regain its normal strength when taken into the caves——

There was the sound of steps and Fred Schroeder came out of the tunnel, dressed as he was dressed in bulky furs. Schroeder looked to the south and said, "It seems to be starting to get a little lighter there."

He saw that it was; a small, faint paling of the black sky.

"They talked over what you and I told them," Schroeder said. "And about how we've struggled to stay here this long and how, even if the sun should stop drifting south this year, it will be years of ice and cold at the caves before Big Spring comes."

"If we leave here the glacier will cover the caves and fill them with ice," he said. "All we ever had will be buried back in there and all we'll have left will be our bows and arrows and animal skins. We'll be taking a one-way road back into the stone age, for ourselves and our children and their children."

"They know that," Schroeder said. "We both told them."

He paused. They watched the sky to the south turn lighter. The

90

northern lights flamed unnoticed behind them as the pale halo of the invisible sun slowly brightened to its maximum. Their faces were white with near-freezing then and they turned to go back into the caves. "They had made their decision," Schroeder went on. "I guess you and I did them an injustice when we thought they had lost their determination, when we thought they might want to hand their children a flint axe and say, 'Here—take this and let it be the symbol of all you are or all you will ever be.'

"Their decision was unanimous—we'll stay for as long as it's possible for us to survive here."

Howard Lake listened to Teacher Morgan West read from the diary of Walter Humbolt, written during the terrible winter of thirty-five years before:

"Each morning the light to the south was brighter. On the seventh morning we saw the sun—and it was not due until the eighth morning!

"It will be years before we can stop fighting the enclosure of the glacier but we have reached and passed the dead of Big Winter. We have reached the bottom and the only direction we can go in the future is up.

"And so," West said, closing the book, "we are here in the caves tonight because of the stubbornness of Humbolt and Schroeder and all the others. Had they thought only of their own welfare, had they conceded defeat and gone into the migratory way of life, we would be sitting beside grass campfires somewhere to the south tonight, our way of life containing no plans or aspirations greater than to follow the game back and forth through the years.

"Now, let's go outside to finish tonight's lesson."

Teacher West led the way into the starlit night just outside the caves, Howard Lake and the other children following him. West pointed to the sky where the star group they called the Athena Constellation blazed like a huge arrowhead high in the east.

"There," he said, "beyond the top of the arrowhead, is where we were going when the Gerns stopped us a hundred and twenty years ago and left us to die on Ragnarok. It's so far that Athena's sun can't be seen from here, so far that it will be another hundred and fifteen years before our first signal gets there. Why is it, then, that you and all the other groups of children have to learn such things as history, physics, the Gern language, and the way to fire a Gern blaster?"

The hand of every child went up. West selected eight-year-old Clifton Humbolt. "Tell us, Clifton," he said.

"Because," Clifton answered, "a Gern cruiser might pass by a few light-years out at any time and pick up our signals. So we have to know all we can about them and how to fight them because there aren't very many of us yet."

"The Gerns will come to kill us," little Marie Chiara said, her dark eyes large and earnest. "They'll come to kill us and to make slaves out of the ones they don't kill, like they did with the others a long time ago. They're awful mean and awful smart and we have to be smarter than they are."

Howard looked again at the Athena constellation, thinking, I hope they come just as soon as I'm old enough to fight them, or even tonight....

"Teacher," he asked, "how would a Gern cruiser look if it came tonight? Would it come from the Athena arrowhead?"

"It probably would," West answered. "You would see its rocket blast, like a bright trail of fire——"

A bright trail of fire burst suddenly into being, coming from the constellation of Athena and lighting up the woods and hills and their startled faces as it arced down toward them.

"It's them!" a treble voice exclaimed and there was a quick flurry of movement as Howard and the other older children shoved the younger children behind them.

Then the light vanished, leaving a dimming glow where it had been.

"Only a meteor," West said. He looked at the line of older children who were standing protectingly in front of the younger ones, rocks in their hands with which to ward off the Gerns, and he smiled in the way he had when he was pleased with them.

Howard watched the meteor trail fade swiftly into invisibility and felt his heartbeats slow from the first wild thrill to gray disappointment. Only a meteor....

But someday he might be leader and by then, surely, the Gerns would come. If not, he would find some way to make them come.

Ten years later Howard Lake was leader. There were three hundred and fifty of them then and Big Spring was on its way to becoming Big Summer. The snow was gone from the southern end of the plateau and once again game migrated up the valleys east of the caves.

There were many things to be done now that Big Winter was past and they could have the chance to do them. They needed a larger pottery kiln, a larger workshop with a wooden lathe, more diamonds to make cutting wheels, more quartz crystals to make binoculars and microscopes. They could again explore the field of inorganic chemistry, even though results in the past had produced nothing of value, and they could, within a few years, resume the metal prospecting up the plateau—the most important project of all.

Their weapons seemed to be as perfect as was possible but when the Gerns came they would need some quick and certain means of communication between the various units that would fight the Gerns. A leader who could not communicate with his forces and coordinate their actions would be helpless. And they had on Ragnarok a form of communication, if trained, that the Gerns could not detect or interfere with electronically: the mockers.

The Craigs were still white and impassable with snow that summer but the snow was receding higher each year. Five years later, in the summer of one hundred and thirty-five, the Craigs were passable for a few weeks.

Lake led a party of eight over them and down into the chasm. They took with them two small cages, constructed of wood and glass and made airtight with the strong medusabush glue. Each cage was equipped with a simple air pump and a pressure gauge.

They brought back two pairs of mockers as interested and trusting captives, together with a supply of the orange corn and a large

93

amount of diamonds. The mockers, in their pressure-maintained cages, were not even aware of the increase in elevation as they were carried over the high summit of the Craigs.

To Lake and the men with him the climb back up the long, steep slope of the mountain was a stiff climb to make in one day but no more than that. It was hard to believe that it had taken Humbolt and Barber almost three days to climb it and that Barber had died in the attempt. It reminded him of the old crossbows that Humbolt and the others had used. They were thin, with a light pull, such as the present generation boys used. It must have required courage for the old ones to dare unicorn attacks with bows so thin that only the small area behind the unicorn's jaws was vulnerable to their arrows....

When the caves were reached, a very gradual reduction of pressure in the mocker cages was started; one that would cover a period of weeks. One pair of mockers survived and had two young ones that fall. The young mockers, like the first generation of Ragnarok-born children of many years before, were more adapted to their environment than their parents were.

The orange corn was planted, using an adaptation method somewhat similar to that used with the mockers. It might have worked had the orange corn not required such a long period of time in which to reach maturity. When winter came only a few grains had formed.

They were saved for next year's seeds, to continue the slow adaptation process.

By the fifth year the youngest generation of mockers was well adapted to the elevation of the caves but for a susceptibility to a quickly fatal form of pneumonia which made it necessary to keep them from exposing themselves to the cold or to any sudden changes of temperature.

Their intelligence was surprising and they seemed to be partially receptive to human thoughts, as Bill Humbolt had written. By the end of the fifteenth year their training had reached such a stage of perfection that a mocker would transmit or not transmit with only the unspoken thought of its master to tell it which it should be. In addition, they would transmit the message to whichever mocker their master's thought directed. Presumably all mockers received the message but only the mocker to whom it was addressed would repeat it aloud.

They had their method of communication. They had their automatic crossbows for quick, close fighting, and their long range longbows. They were fully adapted to the 1.5 gravity and their reflexes were almost like those of prowlers—Ragnarok had long ago separated the quick from the dead.

There were eight hundred and nineteen of them that year, in the early spring of one hundred and fifty, and they were ready and impatient for the coming of the Gerns.

Then the transmitter, which had been in operation again for many years, failed one day.

George Craig had finished checking it when Lake arrived. He looked up from his instruments, remarkably similar in appearance to a sketch of the old George Ord—a resemblance that had been passed down to him by his mother—and said:

"The entire circuit is either gone or ready to go. It's already operated for a lot longer than it should have."

"It doesn't matter," Lake said. "It's served its purpose. We won't rebuild it."

George watched him questioningly.

"It's served its purpose," he said again. "It didn't let us forget that the Gerns will come again. But that isn't enough, now. The first signal won't reach Athena until the year two thirty-five. It will be the dead of Big Winter again then. They'll have to fight the Gerns with bows and arrows that the cold will make as brittle as glass. They won't have a chance."

"No," George said. "They won't have a chance. But what can we do to change it?"

"It's something I've been thinking about," he said. "We'll build a hyperspace transmitter and bring the Gerns before Big Winter comes."

95

"We will?" George asked, lifting his dark eyebrows. "And what do we use for the three hundred pounds of copper and five hundred pounds of iron we would have to have to make the generator?"

"Surely we can find five hundred pounds of iron somewhere on Ragnarok. The north end of the plateau might be the best bet. As for the copper—I doubt that we'll ever find it. But there are seams of a bauxite-like clay in the Western hills—they're certain to contain aluminum to at least some extent. So we'll make the wires of aluminum."

"The ore would have to be refined to pure aluminum oxide before it could be smelted," George said. "And you can't smelt aluminum ore in an ordinary furnace—only in an electric furnace with a generator that can supply a high amperage. And we would have to have cryolite ore to serve as the solvent in the smelting process."

"There's a seam of cryolite in the Eastern Hills, according to the old maps," said Lake. "We could make a larger generator by melting down everything we have. It wouldn't be big enough to power the hyperspace transmitter but it should be big enough to smelt aluminum ore."

George considered the idea. "I think we can do it."

"How long until we can send the signal?" he asked.

"Given the extra metal we need, the building of the generator is a simple job. The transmitter is what will take years—maybe as long as fifty."

Fifty years....

"Can't anything be done to make it sooner?" he asked.

"I know," George said. "You would like for the Gerns to come while you're still here. So would every man on Ragnarok. But even on Earth the building of a hyperspace transmitter was a long, slow job, with all the materials they needed and all the special tools and equipment. Here we'll have to do everything by hand and for materials we have only broken and burned-out odds and ends. It will take about fifty years—it can't be helped."

Fifty years ... but that would bring the Gerns before Big Winter came again. And there was the rapidly increasing chance that a Gern cruiser would at any day intercept the first signals. They were already more than halfway to Athena.

"Melt down the generator," he said. "Start making a bigger one. Tomorrow men will go out after bauxite and cryolite and four of us will go up the plateau to look for iron."

Lake selected Gene Taylor, Tony Chiara and Steve Schroeder to go with him. They were well on their way by daylight the next morning, on the shoulder of each of them a mocker which observed the activity and new scenes with bright, interested eyes.

They traveled light, since they would have fresh meat all the way, and carried herbs and corn only for the mockers. Once, generations before, it had been necessary for men to eat herbs to prevent deficiency diseases but now the deficiency diseases, like Hell Fever, were unknown to them.

They carried no compasses since the radiations of the two suns constantly created magnetic storms that caused compass needles to swing as much as twenty degrees within an hour. Each of them carried a pair of powerful binoculars, however; binoculars that had been diamond-carved from the ivory-like black unicorn horn and set with lenses and prisms of diamond-cut quartz.

The foremost bands of woods goats followed the advance of spring up the plateau and they followed the woods goats. They could not go ahead of the goats—the goats were already pressing close behind the melting of the snow. No hills or ridges were seen as the weeks went by and it seemed to Lake that they would walk forever across the endless rolling floor of the plain.

Early summer came and they walked across a land that was green and pleasantly cool at a time when the vegetation around the caves would be burned brown and lifeless. The woods goats grew less in number then as some of them stopped for the rest of the summer in their chosen latitudes.

They continued on and at last they saw, far to the north, what seemed to be an almost infinitesimal bulge on the horizon. They reached it two days later; a land of rolling green hills, scarred here

97

and there with ragged outcroppings of rock, and a land that climbed slowly and steadily higher as it went into the north.

They camped that night in a little vale. The floor of it was white with the bones of woods goats that had tarried too long the fall before and got caught by an early blizzard. There was still flesh on the bones and scavenger rodents scuttled among the carcasses, feasting.

"We'll split up now," he told the others the next morning.

He assigned each of them his position; Steve Schroeder to parallel his course thirty miles to his right, Gene Taylor to go thirty miles to his left, and Tony Chiara to go thirty miles to the left of Taylor.

"We'll try to hold those distances," he said. "We can't look over the country in detail that way but it will give us a good general survey of it. We don't have too much time left by now and we'll make as many miles into the north as we can each day. The woods goats will tell us when it's time for us to turn back."

They parted company with casual farewells but for Steve Schroeder, who smiled sardonically at the bones of the woods goats in the vale and asked:

"Who's supposed to tell the woods goats?"

Tip, the black, white-nosed mocker on Lake's shoulder, kept twisting his neck to watch the departure of the others until he had crossed the next hill and the others were hidden from view.

"All right, Tip," he said then. "You can unwind your neck now."

"Unwind—all right—all right," Tip said. Then, with a sudden burst of energy which was characteristic of mockers, he began to jiggle up and down and chant in time with his movements, "All right all right all right all right——"

"Shut up!" he commanded. "If you want to talk nonsense I don't care—but don't say 'all right' any more."

"All right," Tip agreed amiably, settling down. "Shut up if you want to talk nonsense. I don't care."

"And don't slaughter the punctuation like that. You change the meaning entirely."

"But don't say all right any more," Tip went on, ignoring him. "You change the meaning entirely."

Then, with another surge of animation, Tip began to fish in his jacket pocket with little hand-like paws. "Tip hungry—Tip hungry."

Lake unbuttoned the pocket and gave Tip a herb leaf. "I notice there's no nonsensical chatter when you want to ask for something to eat."

Tip took the herb leaf but he spoke again before he began to eat; slowly, as though trying seriously to express a thought:

"Tip hungry—no nonsensical."

"Sometimes," he said, turning his head to look at Tip, "you mockers give me the peculiar feeling that you're right on the edge of becoming a new and intelligent race and no fooling."

Tip wiggled his whiskers and bit into the herb leaf. "No fooling," he agreed.

He stopped for the night in a steep-walled hollow and built a small fire of dead moss and grass to ward off the chill that came with dark. He called the others, thinking first of Schroeder so that Tip would transmit to Schroeder's mocker:

"Steve?"

"Here," Tip answered, in a detectable imitation of Schroeder's voice. "No luck."

He thought of Gene Taylor and called, "Gene?"

There was no answer and he called Chiara. "Tony—could you see any of Gene's route today?"

"Part of it," Chiara answered. "I saw a herd of unicorns over that way. Why—doesn't he answer?"

99

"No."

"Then," Chiara said, "they must have got him."

"Did you find anything today, Tony?" he asked.

"Nothing but pure andesite. Not even an iron stain."

It was the same kind of barren formation that he, himself, had been walking over all day. But he had not expected success so soon....

He tried once again to call Gene Taylor:

"Gene ... Gene ... are you there, Gene?"

There was no answer. He knew there would never be.

The days became weeks with dismaying swiftness as they penetrated farther into the north. The hills became more rugged and there were intrusions of granite and other formations to promise a chance of finding metal; a promise that urged them on faster as their time grew shorter.

Twice he saw something white in the distance. Once it was the bones of another band of woods goats that had huddled together and frozen to death in some early blizzard of the past and once it was the bones of a dozen unicorns.

The nights grew chillier and the suns moved faster and faster to the south. The animals began to migrate, an almost imperceptible movement in the beginning but one that increased each day. The first frost came and the migration began in earnest. By the third day it was a hurrying tide.

Tip was strangely silent that day. He did not speak until the noon sun had cleared the cold, heavy mists of morning. When he spoke it was to give a message from Chiara:

"Howard ... last report ... Goldie is dying ... pneumonia...."

Goldie was Chiara's mocker, his only means of communication—and there would be no way to tell him when they were turning back.

"Turn back today, Tony," he said. "Steve and I will go on for a few days more."

There was no answer and he said quickly, "Turn back—turn back! Acknowledge that, Tony."

"Turning back ..." the acknowledgment came. "... tried to save her...."

The message stopped and there was a silence that Chiara's mocker would never break again. He walked on, with Tip sitting very small and quiet on his shoulder. He had crossed another hill before Tip moved, to press up close to him the way mockers did when they were lonely and to hold tightly to him.

"What is it, Tip?" he asked.

"Goldie is dying," Tip said. And then again, like a soft, sad whisper, "Goldie is dying...."

"She was your mate.... I'm sorry."

Tip made a little whimpering sound, and the man reached up to stroke his silky side.

"I'm sorry," he said again. "I'm sorry as hell, little fellow."

For two days Tip sat lonely and silent on his shoulder, no longer interested in the new scenes nor any longer relieving the monotony with his chatter. He refused to eat until the morning of the third day.

By then the exodus of woods goats and unicorns had dwindled to almost nothing; the sky a leaden gray through which the sun could not be seen. That evening he saw what he was sure would be the last band of woods goats and shot one of them.

When he went to it he was almost afraid to believe what he saw.

The hair above its feet was red, discolored with the stain of iron-bearing clay.

He examined it more closely and saw that the goat had apparently

101

watered at a spring where the mud was material washed down from an iron-bearing vein or formation. It had done so fairly recently— there were still tiny particles of clay adhering to the hair.

The wind stirred, cold and damp with its warning of an approaching storm. He looked to the north, where the evening had turned the gray clouds black, and called Schroeder:

"Steve—any luck?"

"None," Schroeder answered.

"I just killed a goat," he said. "It has iron stains on its legs it got at some spring farther north. I'm going on to try to find it. You can turn back in the morning."

"No," Schroeder objected. "I can angle over and catch up with you in a couple of days."

"You'll turn back in the morning," he said. "I'm going to try to find this iron. But if I get caught by a blizzard it will be up to you to tell them at the caves that I found iron and to tell them where it is—you know the mockers can't transmit that far."

There was a short silence; then Schroeder said, "All right—I see. I'll head south in the morning."

Lake took a route the next day that would most likely be the one the woods goats had come down, stopping on each ridge top to study the country ahead of him through his binoculars. It was cloudy all day but at sunset the sun appeared very briefly, to send its last rays across the hills and redden them in mockery of the iron he sought.

Far ahead of him, small even through the glasses and made visible only because of the position of the sun, was a spot at the base of a hill that was redder than the sunset had made the other hills.

He was confident it would be the red clay he was searching for and he hurried on, not stopping until darkness made further progress impossible.

Tip slept inside his jacket, curled up against his chest, while the wind blew raw and cold all through the night. He was on his way again at the first touch of daylight, the sky darker than ever and the wind spinning random flakes of snow before him.

He stopped to look back to the south once, thinking, If I turn back now I might get out before the blizzard hits.

Then the other thought came: These hills all look the same. It I don't go to the iron while I'm this close and know where it is, it might be years before I or anyone else could find it again.

He went on and did not look back again for the rest of the day.

By midafternoon the higher hills around him were hidden under the clouds and the snow was coming harder and faster as the wind drove the flakes against his face. It began to snow with a heaviness that brought a half darkness when he came finally to the hill he had seen through the glasses.

A spring was at the base of it, bubbling out of red clay. Above it the red dirt led a hundred feet to a dike of granite and stopped. He hurried up the hillside that was rapidly whitening with snow and saw the vein.

It set against the dike, short and narrow but red-black with the iron it contained. He picked up a piece and felt the weight of it. It was heavy—it was pure iron oxide.

He called Schroeder and asked, "Are you down out of the high hills, Steve?"

"I'm in the lower ones," Schroeder answered, the words coming a little muffled from where Tip lay inside his jacket. "It looks black as hell up your way."

"I found the iron, Steve. Listen—these are the nearest to landmarks I can give you...."

When he had finished he said, "That's the best I can do. You can't see the red clay except when the sun is low in the southwest but I'm going to build a monument on top of the hill to find it by."

"About you, Howard," Steve asked, "what are your chances?"

The wind was rising to a high moaning around the ledges of the granite dike and the vein was already invisible under the snow.

103

"It doesn't look like they're very good," he answered. "You'll probably be leader when you come back next spring—I told the council I wanted that if anything happened to me. Keep things going the way I would have. Now—I'll have to hurry to get the monument built in time."

"All right," Schroeder said. "So long, Howard ... good luck."

He climbed to the top of the hill and saw boulders there he could use to build the monument. They were large—he might crush Tip against his chest in picking them up—and he took off his jacket, to wrap it around Tip and leave him lying on the ground.

He worked until he was panting for breath, the wind driving the snow harder and harder against him until the cold seemed to have penetrated to the bone. He worked until the monument was too high for his numb hands to lift any more boulders to its top. By then it was tall enough that it should serve its purpose.

He went back to look for Tip, the ground already four inches deep in snow and the darkness almost complete.

"Tip," he called. "Tip—Tip——" He walked back and forth across the hillside in the area where he thought he had left him, stumbling over rocks buried in the snow and invisible in the darkness, calling against the wind and thinking, I can't leave him to die alone here.

Then, from a bulge he had not seen in the snow under him, there came a frightened, lonely wail:

"Tip cold—Tip cold——"

He raked the snow off his jacket and unwrapped Tip, to put him inside his shirt next to his bare skin. Tip's paws were like ice and he was shivering violently, the first symptom of the pneumonia that killed mockers so quickly.

Tip coughed, a wrenching, rattling little sound, and whimpered, "Hurt—hurt——"

"I know," he said. "Your lungs hurt—damn it to hell, I wish I could have let you go home with Steve."

He put on the cold jacket and went down the hill. There was nothing

104

with which he could make a fire—only the short half-green grass, already buried under the snow. He turned south at the bottom of the hill, determining the direction by the wind, and began the stubborn march southward that could have but one ending.

He walked until his cold-numbed legs would carry him no farther. The snow was warm when he fell for the last time; warm and soft as it drifted over him, and his mind was clouded with a pleasant drowsiness.

This isn't so bad, he thought, and there was something like surprise through the drowsiness. I can't regret doing what I had to do—doing it the best I could....

Tip was no longer coughing and the thought of Tip was the only one that was tinged with regret: I hope he wasn't still hurting when he died.

He felt Tip still very feebly against his chest then, and he did not know if it was his imagination or if in that last dreamlike state it was Tip's thought that came to him; warm and close and reassuring him:

No hurt no cold now—all right now—we sleep now....

PART 3

When spring came Steve Schroeder was leader, as Lake had wanted. It was a duty and a responsibility that would be under circumstances different from those of any of the leaders before him. The grim fight was over for a while. They were adapted and increasing in number; going into Big Summer and into a renascence that would last for fifty years. They would have half a century in which to develop their environment to its fullest extent. Then Big Fall would come, to destroy all they had accomplished, and the Gerns would come, to destroy them.

It was his job to make certain that by then they would be stronger than either.

He went north with nine men as soon as the weather permitted. It was hard to retrace the route of the summer before, without compasses, among the hills which looked all the same as far as their binoculars could reach, and it was summer when they saw the hill with the monument. They found Lake's bones a few miles south of it, scattered by the scavengers as were the little bones of his mocker. They buried them together, man and mocker, and went silently on toward the hill.

They had brought a little hand-cranked diamond drill with them to bore holes in the hard granite and black powder for blasting. They mined the vein, sorting out the ore from the waste and saving every particle.

The vein was narrow at the surface and pinched very rapidly. At a depth of six feet it was a knife-blade seam; at ten feet it was only a red discoloration in the bottom of their shaft.

"That seems to be all of it," he said to the others. "We'll send men up here next year to go deeper and farther along its course but I have an idea we've just mined all of the only iron vein on Ragnarok. It will be enough for our purpose."

They sewed the ore in strong rawhide sacks and then prospected,

106

without success, until it was time for the last unicorn band to pass by on its way south. They trapped ten unicorns and hobbled their legs, with other ropes reaching from horn to hind leg on each side to prevent them from swinging back their heads or even lifting them high.

They had expected the capture and hobbling of the unicorns to be a difficult and dangerous job and it was. But when they were finished the unicorns were helpless. They could move awkwardly about to graze but they could not charge. They could only stand with lowered heads and fume and rumble.

The ore sacks were tied on one frosty morning and the men mounted. The horn-leg ropes were loosened so the unicorns could travel, and the unicorns went into a frenzy of bucking and rearing, squealing with rage as they tried to impale their riders.

The short spears, stabbing at the sensitive spot behind the jawbones of the unicorns, thwarted the backward flung heads and the unicorns were slowly forced into submission. The last one conceded temporary defeat and the long journey to the south started, the unicorns going in the run that they could maintain hour after hour.

Each day they pushed the unicorns until they were too weary to fight at night. Each morning, rested, the unicorns resumed the battle. It became an expected routine for both unicorns and men.

The unicorns were released when the ore was unloaded at the foot of the hill before the caves and Schroeder went to the new waterwheel, where the new generator was already in place. There George Craig told him of the unexpected obstacle that had appeared.

"We're stuck," George said. "The aluminum ore isn't what we thought it would be. It's scarce and very low grade, of such a complex nature that we can't refine it to the oxide with what we have to work with on Ragnarok."

"Have you produced any aluminum oxide at all?" Schroeder asked.

"A little. We might have enough for the wire in a hundred years if we kept at it hard enough."

107

"What else do you need—was there enough cryolite?" he asked.

"Not much of it, but enough. We have the generator set up, the smelting box built and the carbon lining and rods ready. We have everything we need to smelt aluminum ore—except the aluminum ore."

"Go ahead and finish up the details, such as installing the lining," he said. "We didn't get this far to be stopped now."

But the prospecting parties, making full use of the time left them before winter closed down, returned late that fall to report no sign of the ore they needed.

Spring came and he was determined they would be smelting aluminum before the summer was over even though he had no idea where the ore would be found. They needed aluminum ore of a grade high enough that they could extract the pure aluminum oxide. Specifically, they needed aluminum oxide....

Then he saw the answer to their problem, so obvious that all of them had overlooked it.

He passed by four children playing a game in front of the caves that day; some kind of a checker-like game in which differently colored rocks represented the different children. One boy was using red stones; some of the rubies that had been brought back as curios from the chasm. Rubies were of no use or value on Ragnarok; only pretty rocks for children to play with....

Only pretty rocks?—rubies and sapphires were corundum, were pure aluminum oxide!

He went to tell George and to arrange for a party of men to go into the chasm after all the rubies and sapphires they could find. The last obstacle had been surmounted.

The summer sun was hot the day the generator hummed into life. The carbon-lined smelting box was ready and the current flowed between the heavy carbon rods suspended in the cryolite and the lining, transforming the cryolite into a liquid. The crushed rubies and sapphires were fed into the box, glowing and glittering in blood-red and sky-blue scintillations of light, to be deprived by the current

108

of their life and fire and be changed into something entirely different.

When the time came to draw off some of the metal they opened the orifice in the lower corner of the box. Molten aluminum flowed out into the ingot mold in a little stream; more beautiful to them than any gems could ever be, bright and gleaming in its promise that more than six generations of imprisonment would soon be ended.

The aluminum smelting continued until the supply of rubies and sapphires in the chasm had been exhausted but for small and scattered fragments. It was enough, with some aluminum above the amount needed for the wire.

It was the year one hundred and fifty-two when they smelted the aluminum. In eight more years they would reach the middle of Big Summer; the suns would start their long drift southward, not to return for one hundred and fifty years. Time was passing swiftly by for them and there was none of it to waste....

The making of ceramics was developed to an art, as was the making of different types of glass. Looms were built to spin thread and cloth from woods goat wool, and vegetable dyes were discovered. Exploration parties crossed the continent to the eastern and western seas: salty and lifeless seas that were bordered by immense deserts. No trees of any kind grew along their shores and ships could not be built to cross them.

Efforts were continued to develop an inorganic field of chemistry, with discouraging results, but in one hundred and fifty-nine the orange corn was successfully adapted to the elevation and climate of the caves.

There was enough that year to feed the mockers all winter, supply next year's seeds, and leave enough that it could be ground and baked into bread for all to taste.

It tasted strange, but good. It was, Schroeder thought, symbolic of a great forward step. It was the first time in generations that any of them had known any food but meat. The corn would make them less dependent upon hunting and, of paramount importance, it was the type of food to which they would have to become accustomed in the

109

future—they could not carry herds of woods goats and unicorns with them on Gern battle cruisers.

The lack of metals hindered them wherever they turned in their efforts to build even the simplest machines or weapons. Despite its dubious prospects, however, they made a rifle-like gun.

The barrel of it was thick, of the hardest, toughest ceramic material they could produce. It was a cumbersome, heavy thing, firing with a flintlock action, and it could not be loaded with much powder lest the charge burst the barrel.

The flintlock ignition was not instantaneous, the lightweight porcelain bullet had far less penetrating power than an arrow, and the thing boomed and belched out a cloud of smoke that would have shown the Gerns exactly where the shooter was located.

It was an interesting curio and the firing of it was something spectacular to behold but it was a weapon apt to be much more dangerous to the man behind it than to the Gern it was aimed at. Automatic crossbows were far better.

Woods goats had been trapped and housed during the summers in shelters where sprays of water maintained a temperature cool enough for them to survive. Only the young were kept when fall came, to be sheltered through the winter in one of the caves. Each new generation was subjected to more heat in the summer and more cold in the winter than the generation before it and by the year one hundred and sixty the woods goats were well on their way toward adaptation.

The next year they trapped two unicorns, to begin the job of adapting and taming future generations of them. If they succeeded they would have utilized the resources of Ragnarok to the limit— except for what should be their most valuable ally with which to fight the Gerns: the prowlers.

For twenty years prowlers had observed a truce wherein they would not go hunting for men if men would stay away from their routes of travel. But it was a truce only and there was no indication that it could ever evolve into friendship.

Three times in the past, half-grown prowlers had been captured and caged in the hope of taming them. Each time they had paced their cages, looking longingly into the distance, refusing to eat and defiant until they died.

To prowlers, as to some men, freedom was more precious than life. And each time a prowler had been captured the free ones had retaliated with a resurgence of savage attacks.

There seemed no way that men and prowlers could ever meet on common ground. They were alien to one another, separated by the gulf of an origin on worlds two hundred and fifty light-years apart. Their only common heritage was the will of each to battle.

But in the spring of one hundred and sixty-one, for a little while one day, the gulf was bridged.

Schroeder was returning from a trip he had taken alone to the east, coming down the long canyon that led from the high face of the plateau to the country near the caves. He hurried, glancing back at the black clouds that had gathered so quickly on the mountain behind him. Thunder rumbled from within them, an almost continuous roll of it as the clouds poured down their deluge of water.

A cloudburst was coming and the sheer-walled canyon down which he hurried had suddenly become a death trap, its sunlit quiet soon to be transformed into roaring destruction. There was only one place along its nine-mile length where he might climb out and the time was already short in which to reach it.

He had increased his pace to a trot when he came to it, a talus of broken rock that sloped up steeply for thirty feet to a shelf. A ledge eleven feet high stood over the shelf and other, lower, ledges set back from it like climbing steps.

At the foot of the talus he stopped to listen, wondering how close behind him the water might be. He heard it coming, a sound like the roaring of a high wind up the canyon, and he scrambled up the talus of loose rock to the shelf at its top. The shelf was not high enough above the canyon's floor—he would be killed there—and he followed it fifty feet around a sharp bend. There it narrowed abruptly, to merge into the sheer wall of the canyon. Blind alley....

111

He ran back to the top of the talus where the edge of the ledge, ragged with projections of rock, was unreachably far above him. As he did so the roaring was suddenly a crashing, booming thunder and he saw the water coming.

It swept around the bend at perhaps a hundred miles an hour, stretching from wall to wall of the canyon, the crest of it seething and slashing and towering forty sheer feet above the canyon's floor.

A prowler was running in front of it, running for its life and losing.

There was no time to watch. He leaped upward, as high as possible, his crossbow in his hand. He caught the end of the bow over one of the sharp projections of rock on the ledge's rim and began to pull himself up, afraid to hurry lest the rock cut the bowstring in two and drop him back.

It held and he stood on the ledge, safe, as the prowler flashed up the talus below.

It darted around the blind-alley shelf and was back a moment later. It saw that its only chance would be to leap up on the ledge where he stood and it tried, handicapped by the steep, loose slope it had to jump from.

It failed and fell back. It tried again, hurling itself upward with all its strength, and its claws caught fleetingly on the rough rock a foot below the rim. It began to slide back, with no time left it for a third try.

It looked up at the rim of safety that it had not quite reached and then on up at him, its eyes bright and cold with the knowledge that it was going to die and its enemy would watch it.

Schroeder dropped flat on his stomach and reached down, past the massive black head, to seize the prowler by the back of the neck. He pulled up with all his strength and the claws of the prowler tore at the rocks as it climbed.

When it was coming up over the ledge, safe, he rolled back from it and came to his feet in one swift, wary motion, his eyes on it and his knife already in his hand. As he did so the water went past below them with a thunder that deafened. Logs and trees shot past,

112

boulders crashed together, and things could be seen surging in the brown depths; shapeless things that had once been woods goats and the battered gray bulk of a unicorn. He saw it all with a sideward glance, his attention on the prowler.

It stepped back from the rim of the ledge and looked at him; warily, as he looked at it. With the wariness was something like question, and almost disbelief.

The ledge they stood on was narrow but it led out of the canyon and to the open land beyond. He motioned to the prowler to precede him and, hesitating a moment, it did so.

They climbed out of the canyon and out onto the grassy slope of the mountainside. The roar of the water was a distant rumble there and he stopped. The prowler did the same and they watched each other again, each of them trying to understand what the thoughts of the other might be. It was something they could not know—they were too alien to each other and had been enemies too long.

Then a gust of wind swept across them, bending and rippling the tall grass, and the prowler swung away to go with it and leave him standing alone.

His route was such that it diverged gradually from that taken by the prowler. He went through a grove of trees and emerged into an open glade on the other side. Up on the ridge to his right he saw something black for a moment, already far away.

He was thirty feet from the next grove of trees when he saw the gray shadow waiting silently for his coming within them.

Unicorn!

His crossbow rattled as he jerked back the pistol grip. The unicorn charged, the underbrush crackling as it tore through it and a vine whipping like a rope from its lowered horn.

His first arrow went into its chest. It lurched, fatally wounded but still coming, and he jerked back on the pistol grip for the quick shot that would stop it.

The rock-frayed bow string broke with a singing sound and the bow ends snapped harmlessly forward.

He had counted on the bow and its failure came a fraction of a second too late for him to dodge far enough. His sideward leap was short, and the horn caught him in midair, ripping across his ribs and breaking them, shattering the bone of his left arm and tearing the flesh. He was hurled fifteen feet and he struck the ground with a stunning impact, pain washing over him in a blinding wave.

Through it, dimly, he saw the unicorn fall and heard its dying trumpet blast as it called to another. He heard an answering call somewhere in the distance and then the faraway drumming of hooves.

He fought back the blindness and used his good arm to lift himself up. His bow was useless, his spear lay broken under the unicorn, and his knife was gone. His left arm swung helplessly and he could not climb the limbless lower trunk of a lance tree with only one arm.

He went forward, limping, trying to hurry to find his knife while the drumming of hooves raced toward him. It would be a battle already lost that he would make with the short knife but he would have blood for his going....

The grass grew tall and thick, hiding the knife until he could hear the unicorn crashing through the trees. He saw it ten feet ahead of him as the unicorn tore out from the edge of the woods thirty feet away.

It squealed, shrill with triumph, and the horn swept up to impale him. There was no time left to reach the knife, no time left for anything but the last fleeting sight of sunshine and glade and arching blue sky——

Something from behind him shot past and up at the unicorn's throat, a thing that was snarling black savagery with yellow eyes blazing and white fangs slashing—the prowler!

It ripped at the unicorn's throat, swerving its charge, and the unicorn plunged past him. The unicorn swung back, all the triumph gone from its squeal, and the prowler struck again. They became a swirling blur, the horn of the unicorn swinging and stabbing and the attacks of the prowler like the swift, relentless thrusting of a rapier.

He went to his knife and when he turned back with it in his hand the battle was already over.

114

The unicorn fell and the prowler turned away from it. One foreleg was bathed in blood and its chest was heaving with a panting so fast that it could not have been caused by the fight with the unicorn.

It must have been watching me, he thought, with a strange feeling of wonder. It was watching from the ridge and it ran all the way.

Its yellow eyes flickered to the knife in his hand. He dropped the knife in the grass and walked forward, unarmed, wanting the prowler to know that he understood; that for them in that moment the gulf of two hundred and fifty light-years did not exist.

He stopped near it and squatted in the grass to begin binding up his broken arm so the bones would not grate together. It watched him, then it began to lick at its bloody shoulder; standing so close to him that he could have reached out and touched it.

Again he felt the sense of wonder. They were alone together in the glade, he and a prowler, each caring for his hurts. There was a bond between them that for a little while made them like brothers. There was a bridge for a little while across the gulf that had never been bridged before....

When he had finished with his arm and the prowler had lessened the bleeding of its shoulder it took a step back toward the ridge. He stood up, knowing it was going to leave.

"I suppose the score is even now," he said to it, "and we'll never see each other again. So good hunting—and thanks."

It made a sound in its throat; a queer sound that was neither bark nor growl, and he had the feeling it was trying to tell him something. Then it turned and was gone like a black shadow across the grass and he was alone again.

He picked up his knife and bow and began the long, painful journey back to the caves, looking again and again at the ridge behind him and thinking: They have a code of ethics. They fight for their survival—but they pay their debts.

Ragnarok was big enough for both men and prowlers. They could live together in friendship as men and dogs of Earth lived together. It might take a long time to win the trust of the prowlers but surely it could be done.

115

He came to the rocky trail that led to the caves and there he took a last look at the ridge behind him; feeling a poignant sense of loss and wondering if he would ever see the prowler again or ever again know the strange, wild companionship he had known that day.

Perhaps he never would ... but the time would come on Ragnarok when children would play in the grass with prowler pups and the time would come when men and prowlers, side by side, would face the Gerns.

In the year that followed there were two incidents when a prowler had the opportunity to kill a hunter on prowler territory and did not do so. There was no way of knowing if the prowler in each case had been the one he had saved from the cloudburst or if the prowlers, as a whole, were respecting what a human had done for one of them.

Schroeder thought of again trying to capture prowler pups—very young ones—and decided it would be a stupid plan. Such an act would destroy all that had been done toward winning the trust of the prowlers. It would be better to wait, even though time was growing short, and find some other way.

The fall of one hundred and sixty-three came and the suns were noticeably moving south. That was the fall that his third child, a girl, was born. She was named Julia, after the Julia of long ago, and she was of the last generation that would be born in the caves.

Plans were already under way to build a town in the valley a mile from the caves. The unicorn-proof stockade wall that would enclose it was already under construction, being made of stone blocks. The houses would be of diamond-sawed stone, thick-walled, with dead-air spaces between the double walls to insulate against heat and cold. Tall, wide canopies of lance tree poles and the palm-like medusabush leaves would be built over all the houses to supply additional shade.

The woods goats were fully adapted that year and domesticated to such an extent that they had no desire to migrate with the wild goats. There was a small herd of them then, enough to supply a limited amount of milk, cheese and wool.

The adaptation of the unicorns proceeded in the following years, but not their domestication. It was their nature to be ill-tempered and treacherous and only the threat of the spears in the hands of their drivers forced them to work; work that they could have done easily had they not diverted so much effort each day to trying to turn on their masters and kill them. Each night they were put in a massive-walled corral, for they were almost as dangerous as wild unicorns.

The slow, painstaking work on the transmitter continued while the suns moved farther south each year. The move from the caves to the new town was made in one hundred and seventy-nine, the year that Schroeder's wife died.

His two sons were grown and married and Julia, at sixteen, was a woman by Ragnarok standards; blue-eyed and black-haired as her mother, a Craig, had been, and strikingly pretty in a wild, reckless way. She married Will Humbolt that spring, leaving her father alone in the new house in the new town.

Four months later she came to him to announce with pride and excitement:

"I'm going to have a baby in only six months! If it's a boy he'll be the right age to be leader when the Gerns come and we're going to name him John, after the John who was the first leader we ever had on Ragnarok."

Her words brought to his mind a question and he thought of what old Dale Craig, the leader who had preceded Lake, had written:

We have survived, the generations that the Gerns thought would never be born. But we must never forget the characteristics that insured that survival: an unswerving loyalty of every individual to all the others and the courage to fight, and die if necessary.

In any year, now, the Gerns will come. There will be no one to help us. Those on Athena are slaves and it is probable that Earth has been enslaved by now. We will stand or fall alone. But if we of today could know that the ones who meet the Gerns will still have the courage and loyalty that made our survival possible, then we would know that the Gerns are already defeated....

The era of danger and violence was over for a little while. The younger generation had grown up during a time of peaceful

117

development of their environment. It was a peace that the coming of the Gerns would shatter—but had it softened the courage and loyalty of the younger generation?

A week later he was given his answer.

He was climbing up the hill that morning, high above the town below, when he saw the blue of Julia's wool blouse in the distance. She was sitting up on a hillside, an open book in her lap and her short spear lying beside her.

He frowned at the sight. The main southward migration of unicorns was over but there were often lone stragglers who might appear at any time. He had warned her that someday a unicorn would kill her—but she was reckless by nature and given to restless moods in which she could not stand the confinement of the town.

She jerked up her head as he watched, as though at a faint sound, and he saw the first movement within the trees behind her—a unicorn.

It lunged forward, its stealth abandoned as she heard it, and she came to her feet in a swift, smooth movement; the spear in her hand and the book spilling to the ground.

The unicorn's squeal rang out and she whirled to face it, with two seconds to live. He reached for his bow, knowing his help would come too late.

She did the only thing possible that might enable her to survive: she shifted her balance to take advantage of the fact that a human could jump to one side a little more quickly than a four-footed beast in headlong charge. As she did so she brought up the spear for the thrust into the vulnerable area just behind the jawbone.

It seemed the needle point of the black horn was no more than an arm's length from her stomach when she jumped aside with the lithe quickness of a prowler, swinging as she jumped and thrusting the spear with all her strength into the unicorn's neck.

The thrust was true and the spear went deep. She released it and flung herself backward to dodge the flying hooves. The force of the unicorn's charge took it past her but its legs collapsed under it and it crashed to the ground, sliding a little way before it stopped. It kicked once and lay still.

She went to it, to retrieve her spear, and even from the distance there was an air of pride about her as she walked past her bulky victim.

Then she saw the book, knocked to one side by the unicorn's hooves. Tatters of its pages were blowing in the wind and she stiffened, her face growing pale. She ran to it to pick it up, the unicorn forgotten.

She was trying to smooth the torn leaves when he reached her. It had been one of the old textbooks, printed on real paper, and it was fragile with age. She had been trusted by the librarian to take good care of it. Now, page after page was torn and unreadable....

She looked up at him, shame and misery on her face.

"Father," she said. "The book—I——"

He saw that the unicorn was a bull considerably larger than the average. Men had in the past killed unicorns with spears but never, before, had a sixteen-year-old girl done so....

He looked back at her, keeping his face emotionless, and asked sternly, "You what?"

"I guess—I guess I didn't have any right to take the book out of town. I wish I hadn't...."

"You promised to take good care of it," he told her coldly. "Your promise was believed and you were trusted to keep it."

"But—but I didn't mean to damage it—I didn't mean to!" She was suddenly very near to tears. "I'm not a—a bemmon!"

"Go back to town," he ordered. "Tonight bring the book to the town hall and tell the council what happened to it."

She swallowed and said in a faint voice, "Yes, father."

She turned and started slowly back down the hill, not seeing the unicorn as she passed it, the bloody spear trailing disconsolately behind her and her head hanging in shame.

119

He watched her go and it was safe for him to smile. When night came and she stood before the council, ashamed to lift her eyes to look at them, he would have to be grim and stern as he told her how she had been trusted and how she had betrayed that trust. But now, as he watched her go down the hill, he could smile with his pride in her and know that his question was answered; that the younger generation had lost neither courage nor loyalty.

Julia saved a child's life that spring and almost lost her own. The child was playing under a half-completed canopy when a sudden, violent wind struck it and transformed it into a death-trap of cracking, falling timbers. She reached him in time to fling him to safety but the collapsing roof caught her before she could make her own escape.

Her chest and throat were torn by the jagged ends of the broken poles and for a day and a night her life was a feebly flickering spark. She began to rally on the second night and on the third morning she was able to speak for the first time, her eyes dark and tortured with her fear:

"My baby—what did it do to him?"

She convalesced slowly, haunted by the fear. Her son was born five weeks later and her fears proved to have been groundless. He was perfectly normal and healthy.

And hungry—and her slowly healing breasts would be dry for weeks to come.

By a coincidence that had never happened before and could never happen again there was not a single feeding-time foster-mother available for the baby. There were many expectant mothers but only three women had young babies—and each of the three had twins to feed.

But there was a small supply of frozen goat milk in the ice house, enough to see young Johnny through until it was time for the goat herd to give milk. He would have to live on short rations until then but it could not be helped.

Johnny was a month old when the opportunity came for the men of Ragnarok to have their ultimate ally.

The last of the unicorns were going north and the prowlers had long since gone. The blue star was lighting the night like a small sun when the breeze coming through Schroeder's window brought the distant squealing of unicorns.

He listened, wondering. It was a sound that did not belong. Everyone was safely in the town, most of them in bed, and there should be nothing outside the stockade for the unicorns to fight.

He armed himself with spear and crossbow and went outside. He let himself out through the east gate and went toward the sounds of battle. They grew louder as he approached, more furious, as though the battle was reaching its climax.

He crossed the creek and went through the trees beyond. There, in a small clearing no more than half a mile from the town, he came upon the scene.

A lone prowler was making a stand against two unicorns. Two other unicorns lay on the ground, dead, and behind the prowler was the dark shape of its mate lying lifelessly in the grass. There was blood on the prowler, purple in the blue starlight, and gloating rang in the squeals of the unicorns as they lunged at it. The leaps of the prowler were faltering as it fought them, the last desperate defiance of an animal already dying.

He brought up the bow and sent a volley of arrows into the unicorns. Their gloating squeals died and they fell. The prowler staggered and fell beside them.

It was breathing its last when he reached it but in the way it looked up at him he had the feeling that it wanted to tell him something, that it was trying hard to live long enough to do so. It died with the strange appeal in its eyes and not until then did he see the scar on its shoulder; a scar such as might have been made long ago by the rip of a unicorn's horn.

It was the prowler he had known nineteen years before.

The ground was trampled all around by the unicorns, showing that the prowlers had been besieged all day. He went to the other prowler and saw it was a female. Her breasts showed that she had had pups recently but she had been dead at least two days. Her hind

121

legs had been broken sometime that spring and they were still only half healed, twisted and almost useless.

Then, that was why the two of them were so far behind the other prowlers. Prowlers, like the wolves, coyotes and foxes of Earth, mated for life and the male helped take care of the young. She had been injured somewhere to the south, perhaps in a fight with unicorns, and her mate had stayed with her as she hobbled her slow way along and killed game for her. The pups had been born and they had had to stop. Then the unicorns had found them and the female had been too crippled to fight....

He looked for the pups, expecting to find them trampled and dead. But they were alive, hidden under the roots of a small tree near their mother.

Prowler pups—alive!

They were very young, small and blind and helpless. He picked them up and his elation drained away as he looked at them. They made little sounds of hunger, almost inaudible, and they moved feebly, trying to find their mother's breasts and already so weak that they could not lift their heads.

Small chunks of fresh meat had been left beside the pups and he thought of what the prowler's emotions must have been as his mate lay dead on the ground and he carried meat to their young, knowing they were too small to eat it but helpless to do anything else for them.

And he knew why there had been the appeal in the eyes of the prowler as it died and what it had tried to tell him: Save them ... as you once saved me.

He carried the pups back past the prowler and looked down at it in passing. "I'll do my best," he said.

When he reached his house he laid the pups on his bed and built a fire. There was no milk to give them—the goats would not have young for at least another two weeks—but perhaps they could eat a soup of some kind. He put water on to boil and began shredding meat to make them a rich broth.

One of them was a male, the other a female, and if he could save

122

them they would fight beside the men of Ragnarok when the Gerns came. He thought of what he would name them as he worked. He would name the female Sigyn, after Loki's faithful wife who went with him when the gods condemned him to Hel, the Teutonic underworld. And he would name the male Fenrir, after the monster wolf who would fight beside Loki when Loki led the forces of Hel in the final battle on the day of Ragnarok.

But when the broth was prepared, and cooled enough, the pups could not eat it. He tried making it weaker, tried it mixed with corn and herb soup, tried corn and herb soups alone. They could eat nothing he prepared for them.

When gray daylight entered the room he had tried everything possible and had failed. He sat wearily in his chair and watched them, defeated. They were no longer crying in their hunger and when he touched them they did not move as they had done before.

They would be dead before the day was over and the only chance men had ever had to have prowlers as their friends and allies would be gone.

The first rays of sunrise were coming into the room, revealing fully the frail thinness of the pups, when there was a step outside and Julia's voice:

"Father?"

"Come in, Julia," he said, not moving.

She entered, still a pale shadow of the reckless girl who had fought a unicorn, even though she was slowly regaining her normal health. She carried young Johnny in one arm, in her other hand his little bottle of milk. Johnny was hungry—there was never quite enough milk for him—but he was not crying. Ragnarok children did not cry....

She saw the pups and her eyes went wide.

"Prowlers—baby prowlers! Where did you get them?"

He told her and she went to them, to look down at them and say, "If you and their father hadn't helped each other that day they wouldn't be here, nor you, nor I, nor Johnny—none of us in this room."

"They won't live out the day," he said. "They have to have milk—and there isn't any."

She reached down to touch them and they seemed to sense that she was someone different. They stirred, making tiny whimpering sounds and trying to move their heads to nuzzle at her fingers.

Compassion came to her face, like a soft light.

"They're so young," she said. "So terribly young to have to die...."

She looked at Johnny and at the little bottle that held his too-small morning ration of milk.

"Johnny—Johnny——" Her words were almost a whisper. "You're hungry—but we can't let them die. And someday, for this, they will fight for your life."

She sat on the bed and placed the pups in her lap beside Johnny. She lifted a little black head with gentle fingers and a little pink mouth ceased whimpering as it found the nipple of Johnny's bottle.

Johnny's gray eyes darkened with the storm of approaching protest. Then the other pup touched his hand, crying in its hunger, and the protest faded as surprise and something like sudden understanding came into his eyes.

Julia withdrew the bottle from the first pup and transferred it to the second one. Its crying ceased and Johnny leaned forward to touch it again, and the one beside it.

He made his decision with an approving sound and leaned back against his mother's shoulder, patiently awaiting his own turn and their presence accepted as though they had been born his brother and sister.

The golden light of the new day shone on them, on his daughter and grandson and the prowler pups, and in it he saw the bright omen for the future.

His own role was nearing its end but he had seen the people of Ragnarok conquer their environment in so far as Big Winter would ever let it be conquered. The last generation was being born, the generation that would meet the Gerns, and now they would have their final ally. Perhaps it would be Johnny who led them on that day, as the omen seemed to prophesy.

He was the son of a line of leaders, born to a mother who had fought and killed a unicorn. He had gone hungry to share what little he had with the young of Ragnarok's most proud and savage species and Fenrir and Sigyn would fight beside him on the day he led the forces of the hell-world in the battle with the Gerns who thought they were gods.

Could the Gerns hope to have a leader to match?

PART 4

John Humbolt, leader, stood on the wide stockade wall and watched
the lowering sun touch the western horizon—far south of where it
had set when he was a child. Big Summer was over and now, in the
year two hundred, they were already three years into Big Fall. The
Craigs had been impassable with snow for five years and the country
at the north end of the plateau, where the iron had been found, had
been buried under never-melting snow and growing glaciers for
twenty years.

There came the soft tinkling of ceramic bells as the herd of milk
goats came down off the hills. Two children were following and six
prowlers walked with them, to protect them from wild unicorns.

There were not many of the goats. Each year the winters were
longer, requiring the stocking of a larger supply of hay. The time
would come when the summers would be so short and the winters
so long that they could not keep goats at all. And by then, when Big
Winter had closed in on them, the summer seasons would be too
short for the growing of the orange corn. They would have nothing
left but the hunting.

They had, he knew, reached and passed the zenith of the
development of their environment. From a low of forty-nine men,
women and children in dark caves they had risen to a town of six
thousand. For a few years they had had a way of life that was almost
a civilization but the inevitable decline was already under way. The
years of frozen sterility of Big Winter were coming and no amount
of determination or ingenuity could alter them. Six thousand would
have to live by hunting—and one hundred, in the first Big Winter,
had found barely enough game.

They would have to migrate in one of two different ways: they could
go to the south as nomad hunters—or they could go to other, fairer,
worlds in ships they took from the Gerns.

The choice was very easy to make and they were almost ready.

In the workshop at the farther edge of town the hyperspace

transmitter was nearing completion. The little smelter was waiting to receive the lathe and other iron and steel and turn them into the castings for the generator. Their weapons were ready, the mockers were trained, the prowlers were waiting. And in the massive corral beyond town forty half-tame unicorns trampled the ground and hated the world, wanting to kill something. They had learned to be afraid of Ragnarok men but they would not be afraid to kill Gerns....

The children with the goats reached the stockade and two of the prowlers, Fenrir and Sigyn, turned to see him standing on the wall. He made a little motion with his hand and they came running, to leap up beside him on the ten-foot-high wall.

"So you've been checking up on how well the young ones guard the children?" he asked.

Sigyn lolled out her tongue and her white teeth grinned at him in answer. Fenrir, always the grimmer of the two, made a sound in his throat in reply.

Prowlers developed something like a telepathic rapport with their masters and could sense their thoughts and understand relatively complex instructions. Their intelligence was greater, and of a far more mature order, than that of the little mockers but their vocal cords were not capable of making the sounds necessary for speech.

He rested his hands on their shoulders, where their ebony fur was frosted with gray. Age had not yet affected their quick, flowing movement but they were getting old—they were only a few weeks short of his own age. He could not remember when they had not been with him....

Sometimes it seemed to him he could remember those hungry days when he and Fenrir and Sigyn shared together in his mother's lap—but it was probably only his imagination from having heard the story told so often. But he could remember for certain when he was learning to walk and Fenrir and Sigyn, full grown then, walked tall and black beside him. He could remember playing with Sigyn's pups and he could remember Sigyn watching over them all, sometimes giving her pups a bath and his face a washing with equal disregard for their and his protests. Above all he could remember the times when he was almost grown; the wild, free days when he and Fenrir and Sigyn had roamed the mountains together. With a bow and a

127

knife and two prowlers beside him he had felt that there was nothing on Ragnarok that they could not conquer; that there was nothing in the universe they could not defy together....

There was a flicker of black movement and a young messenger prowler came running from the direction of the council hall, a speckle-faced mocker clinging to its back. It leaped up on the wall beside him and the mocker, one that had been trained to remember and repeat messages verbatim, took a breath so deep that its cheeks bulged out. It spoke, in a quick rush like a child that is afraid it might forget some of the words:

"You will please come to the council hall to lead the discussion regarding the last preparations for the meeting with the Gerns. The transmitter is completed."

The lathe was torn down the next day and the smelter began to roar with its forced draft. Excitement and anticipation ran through the town like a fever. It would take perhaps twenty days to build the generator, working day and night so that not an hour of time would be lost, forty days for the signal to reach Athena, and forty days for the Gern cruiser to reach Ragnarok——

In one hundred days the Gerns would be there!

The men who would engage in the fight for the cruiser quit trimming their beards. Later, when it was time for the Gerns to appear, they would discard their woolen garments for ones of goat skin. The Gerns would regard them as primitive inferiors at best and it might be of advantage to heighten the impression. It would make the awakening of the Gerns a little more shocking.

An underground passage, leading from the town to the concealment of the woods in the distance, had long ago been dug. Through it the women and children would go when the Gerns arrived.

There was a level area of ground, just beyond the south wall of town, where the cruiser would be almost certain to land. The town had been built with that thought in mind. Woods were not far from both sides of the landing site and unicorn corrals were hidden in them. From the corrals would come the rear flanking attack against the Gerns.

128

The prowlers, of course, would be scattered among all the forces.

The generator was completed and installed on the nineteenth night. Charley Craig, a giant of a man whose red beard gave him a genially murderous appearance, opened the valve of the water pipe. The new wooden turbine stirred and belts and pulleys began to spin. The generator hummed, the needles of the dials climbed, flickered, and steadied.

Norman Lake looked from them to Humbolt, his pale gray eyes coldly satisfied. "Full output," he said. "We have the power we need this time."

Jim Chiara was at the transmitter and they waited while he threw switches and studied dials. Every component of the transmitter had been tested but they had not had the power to test the complete assembly.

"That's it," he said at last, looking up at them. "She's ready, after almost two hundred years of wanting her."

Humbolt wondered what the signal should be and saw no reason why it should not be the same one that had been sent out with such hope a hundred and sixty-five years ago.

"All right, Jim," he said. "Let the Gerns know we're waiting for them—make it 'Ragnarok calling' again."

The transmitter key rattled and the all-wave signal that the Gerns could not fail to receive went out at a velocity of five light-years a day:

Ragnarok calling—Ragnarok calling—Ragnarok calling—

It was the longest summer Humbolt had ever experienced. He was not alone in his impatience—among all of them the restlessness flamed higher as the slow days dragged by, making it almost impossible to go about their routine duties. The gentle mockers sensed the anticipation of their masters for the coming battle and they became nervous and apprehensive. The prowlers sensed it and they paced about the town in the dark of night; watching, listening, on ceaseless guard against the mysterious enemy their masters

129

waited for. Even the unicorns seemed to sense what was coming and they rumbled and squealed in their corrals at night, red-eyed with the lust for blood and sometimes attacking the log walls with blows that shook the ground.

The interminable days went their slow succession and summer gave way to fall. The hundredth day dawned, cold and gray with the approach of winter; the day of the Gerns.

But no cruiser came that day, nor the next. He stood again on the stockade wall in the evening of the third day, Fenrir and Sigyn beside him. He listened for the first dim, distant sound of the Gern cruiser and heard only the moaning of the wind around him.

Winter was coming. Always, on Ragnarok, winter was coming or the brown death of summer. Ragnarok was a harsh and barren prison, and no amount of desire could ever make it otherwise. Only the coming of a Gern cruiser could ever offer them the bloody, violent opportunity to regain their freedom.

But what if the cruiser never came?

It was a thought too dark and hopeless to be held. They were not asking a large favor of fate, after two hundred years of striving for it; only the chance to challenge the Gern Empire with bows and knives....

Fenrir stiffened, the fur lifting on his shoulders and a muted growl coming from him. Then Humbolt heard the first whisper of sound; a faint, faraway roaring that was not the wind.

He watched and listened and the sound came swiftly nearer, rising in pitch and swelling in volume. Then it broke through the clouds, tall and black and beautifully deadly. It rode down on its rockets of flame, filling the valley with its thunder, and his heart hammered with exultation.

It had come—the cruiser had come!

He turned and dropped the ten feet to the ground inside the stockade. The warning signal was being sounded from the center of town; a unicorn horn that gave out the call they had used in the practice alarms. Already the women and children would be hurrying

130

along the tunnels that led to the temporary safety of the woods beyond town. The Gerns might use their turret blasters to destroy the town and all in it before the night was over. There was no way of knowing what might happen before it ended. But whatever it was, it would be the action they had all been wanting.

He ran to where the others would be gathering, Fenrir and Sigyn loping beside him and the horn ringing wild and savage and triumphant as it announced the end of two centuries of waiting.

The cruiser settled to earth in the area where it had been expected to land, towering high above the town with its turret blasters looking down upon the houses.

Charley Craig and Norman Lake were waiting for him on the high steps of his own house in the center of town where the elevation gave them a good view of the ship yet where the fringes of the canopy would conceal them from the ship's scanners. They were heavily armed, their prowlers beside them and their mockers on their shoulders.

Elsewhere, under the connected rows of concealing canopies, armed men were hurrying to their prearranged stations. Most of them were accompanied by prowlers, bristling and snarling as they looked at the alien ship. A few men were deliberately making themselves visible not far away, going about unimportant tasks with only occasional and carefully disinterested glances toward the ship. They were the bait, to lure the first detachment into the center of town....

"Well?" Norman Lake asked, his pale eyes restless with his hunger for violence. "There's our ship—when do we take her?"

"Just as soon as we get them outside it," he said. "We'll use the plan we first had—wait until they send a full force to rescue the first detachment and then hit them with everything we have."

His black, white-nosed mocker was standing in the open doorway and watching the hurrying men and prowlers with worried interest: Tip, the great-great-great-great grandson of the mocker that had died with Howard Lake north of the plateau. He reached down to pick him up and set him on his shoulder, and said:

"Jim?"

131

"The longbows are ready," Tip's treble imitation of Jim Chiara's voice answered. "We'll black out their searchlights when the time comes."

"Andy?" he asked.

"The last of us for this section are coming in now," Andy Taylor answered.

He made his check of all the subleaders, then looked up to the roof to ask, "All set, Jimmy?"

Jimmy Stevens' grinning face appeared over the edge. "Ten crossbows are cocked and waiting up here. Bring us our targets."

They waited, while the evening deepened into near-dusk. Then the airlock of the cruiser slid open and thirteen Gerns emerged, the one leading them wearing the resplendent uniform of a subcommander.

"There they come," he said to Lake and Craig. "It looks like we'll be able to trap them in here and force the commander to send out a full-sized force. We'll all attack at the sound of the horn and if you can hit their rear flanks hard enough with the unicorns to give us a chance to split them from this end some of us should make it to the ship before they realize up in the control room that they should close the airlocks.

"Now"—he looked at the Gerns who were coming straight toward the stockade wall, ignoring the gate to their right—"you'd better be on your way. We'll meet again before long in the ship."

Fenrir and Sigyn looked from the advancing Gerns to him with question in their eyes after Lake and Craig were gone, Fenrir growling restlessly.

"Pretty soon," he said to them. "Right now it would be better if they didn't see you. Wait inside, both of you." They went reluctantly inside, to merge with the darkness of the interior. Only an occasional yellow gleam of their eyes showed that they were crouched to spring just inside the doorway.

He called to the nearest unarmed man, not loud enough to be heard by the Gerns:

"Cliff—you and Sam Anders come here. Tell the rest to fade out of sight and get armed."

Cliff Schroeder passed the command along and he and Sam Anders approached. He looked back at the Gerns and saw they were within a hundred feet of the—for them—unscalable wall of the stockade. They were coming without hesitation——

A pale blue beam lashed down from one of the cruiser's turrets and a fifty foot section of the wall erupted into dust with a sound like thunder. The wind swept the dust aside in a gigantic cloud and the Gerns came through the gap, looking neither to right nor left.

"That, I suppose," Sam Anders said from beside him, "was Lesson Number One for degenerate savages like us: Gerns, like gods, are not to be hindered by man-made barriers."

The Gerns walked with a peculiar gait that puzzled him until he saw what it was. They were trying to come with the arrogant military stride affected by the Gerns and in the 1.5 gravity they were succeeding in achieving only a heavy clumping.

They advanced steadily and as they drew closer he saw that in the right hand of each Gern soldier was a blaster while in the left hand of each could be seen the metallic glitter of chains.

Schroeder smiled thinly. "It looks like they want to subject about a dozen of us to some painful questioning."

No one else was any longer in sight and the Gerns came straight toward the three on the steps. They stopped forty feet away at a word of command from the officer and Gerns and Ragnarok men exchanged silent stares; the faces of the Ragnarok men bearded and expressionless, the faces of the Gerns hairless and reflecting a contemptuous curiosity.

"Narth!" The communicator on the Gern officer's belt spoke with metallic authority. "What do they look like? Did we come two hundred light-years to view some animated vegetables?"

"No, Commander," Narth answered. "I think the discard of the Rejects two hundred years ago has produced for us an unexpected reward. There are three natives under the canopy before me and

133

their physical perfection and complete adaptation to this hellish gravity is astonishing."

"They could be used to replace expensive machines on some of the outer world mines," the commander said, "providing their intelligence isn't too abysmally low. What about that?"

"They can surely be taught to perform simple manual labor," Narth answered.

"Get on with your job," the commander said. "Try to pick some of the most intelligent looking ones for questioning—I can't believe these cattle sent that message and they're going to tell us who did. And pick some young, strong ones for the medical staff to examine—ones that won't curl up and die after the first few cuts of the knife."

"We'll chain these three first," Narth said. He lifted his hand in an imperious gesture to Humbolt and the other two and ordered in accented Terran: "Come here!"

No one moved and he said again, sharply, "Come here!"

Again no one moved and the minor officer beside Narth said, "Apparently they can't even understand Terran now."

"Then we'll give them some action they can understand," Narth snapped, his face flushing with irritation. "We'll drag them out by their heels!"

The Gerns advanced purposefully, three of them holstering their blasters to make their chains ready. When they had passed under the canopy and could not be seen from the ship Humbolt spoke:

"All right, Jimmy."

The Gerns froze in midstride, suspicion flashing across their faces.

"Look up on the roof," he said in Gern.

They looked, and the suspicion became gaping dismay.

"You can be our prisoners or you can be corpses," he said. "We don't care which."

The urgent hiss of Narth's command broke their indecision:

"Kill them!"

Six of them tried to obey, bringing up their blasters in movements that seemed curiously heavy and slow, as though the gravity of Ragnarok had turned their arms to wood. Three of them almost lifted their blasters high enough to fire at the steps in front of them before arrows went through their throats. The other three did not get that far.

Narth and the remaining six went rigidly motionless and he said to them:

"Drop your blasters—quick!"

Their blasters thumped to the ground and Jimmy Stevens and his bowmen slid off the roof. Within a minute the Gerns were bound with their own chains, but for the officer, and the blasters were in the hands of the Ragnarok men.

Jimmy looked down the row of Gerns and shook his head. "So these are Gerns?" he said. "It was like trapping a band of woods goats."

"Young ones," Schroeder amended. "And almost as dangerous."

Narth's face flushed at the words and his eyes went to the ship. The sight of it seemed to restore his courage and his lips drew back in a snarl.

"You fools—you stupid, megalomaniac dung-heaps—do you think you can kill Gerns and live to boast about it?"

"Keep quiet," Humbolt ordered, studying him with curiosity. Narth, like all the Gerns, was different from what they had expected. It was true the Gerns had strode into their town with an attempt at arrogance but they were harmless in appearance, soft of face and belly, and the snarling of the red-faced Narth was like the bluster of a cornered scavenger-rodent.

"I promise you this," Narth was saying viciously, "if you don't release us and return our weapons this instant I'll personally oversee the extermination of you and every savage in this village

135

with the most painful death science can contrive and I'll——"

Humbolt reached out his hand and flicked Narth under the chin. Narth's teeth cracked loudly together and his face twisted with the pain of a bitten tongue.

"Tie him up, Jess," he said to a man near him. "If he opens his mouth again, shove your foot in it."

He spoke to Schroeder. "We'll keep three of the blasters and send two to each of the other front groups. Have that done."

Dusk was deepening into darkness and he called Chiara again. "They'll turn on their searchlights any minute and make the town as light as day," he said. "If you can keep them blacked out until some of us have reached the ship, I think we'll have won."

"They'll be kept blacked out," Chiara said. "With some flint-headed arrows left over for the Gerns."

He called Lake and Craig, to be told they were ready and waiting.

"But we're having hell keeping the unicorns quiet," Craig said. "They want to get to killing something."

He pressed the switch of the communicator but it was dead. They had, of course, transferred to some other wave length so he could not hear the commands. It was something he had already anticipated....

Fenrir and Sigyn were still obediently inside the doorway, almost frantic with desire to rejoin him. He spoke to them and they bounded out, snarling at three Gerns in passing and causing them to blanch to a dead-white color.

He set Tip on Sigyn's shoulders and said, "Sigyn, there's a job for you and Tip to do. A dangerous job. Listen—both of you...."

The yellow eyes of Sigyn and the dark eyes of the little mocker looked into his as he spoke to them and accompanied his words with the strongest, clearest mental images he could project:

"Sigyn, take Tip to the not-men thing. Leave him hidden in the grass

136

to one side of the big hole in it. Tip, you wait there. When the not-men come out you listen, and tell what they say.

"Now, do you both understand?"

Sigyn made a sound that meant she did but Tip clutched at his wrist with little paws suddenly gone cold and wailed, "No! Scared—scared——"

"You have to go, Tip," he said, gently disengaging his wrist. "And Sigyn will hide near to you and watch over you." He spoke to Sigyn. "When the horn calls you run back with him."

Again she made the sound signifying understanding and he touched them both in what he hoped would not be the last farewell.

"All right, Sigyn—go now."

She vanished into the gloom of coming night, Tip hanging tightly to her. Fenrir stood with the fur lifted on his shoulders and a half snarl on his face as he watched her go and watched the place where the not-men would appear.

"Where's Freckles?" he asked Jimmy.

"Here," someone said, and came forward with Tip's mate.

He set Freckles on his shoulder and the first searchlight came on, shining down from high up on the cruiser. It lighted up the area around them in harsh white brilliance, its reflection revealing the black shadow that was Sigyn just vanishing behind the ship.

Two more searchlights came on, to illuminate the town. Then the Gerns came.

They poured out through the airlock and down the ramp, there to form in columns that marched forward as still more Gerns hurried down the ramp behind them. The searchlights gleamed on their battle helmets and on the blades of the bayonets affixed to their rifle-like long range blasters. Hand blasters and grenades hung from their belts, together with stubby flame guns.

They were a solid mass reaching halfway to the stockade before the last of them, the commanding officers, appeared. One of them

137

stopped at the foot of the ramp to watch the advance of the punitive force and give the frightened but faithful Tip the first words to transmit to Freckles:

"The full force is on its way, Commander."

A reply came, in Freckles' simulation of the metallic tones of a communicator:

"The key numbers of the confiscated blasters have been checked and the disturbance rays of the master integrator set. You'll probably have few natives left alive to take as prisoners after those thirteen charges explode but continue with a mopping up job that the survivors will never forget."

So the Gerns could, by remote control, set the total charges of stolen blasters to explode upon touching the firing stud? It was something new since the days of the Old Ones....

He called Chiara and the other groups, quickly, to tell them what he had learned. "We'll get more blasters—ones they can't know the numbers of—when we attack," he finished.

He took the blaster from his belt and laid it on the ground. The front ranks of the Gerns were almost to the wall by then, a column wider than the gap that had been blasted through it, coming with silent purposefulness.

Two blaster beams lanced down from the turrets, to smash at the wall. Dust billowed and thunder rumbled as they swept along. A full three hundred feet of the wall had been destroyed when they stopped and the dust hid the ship and made dim glows of the searchlights.

It had no doubt been intended to impress them with the might of the Gerns but in doing so it hid the Ragnarok forces from the advancing Gerns for a few seconds.

"Jim—black out their lights before the dust clears," he called. "Joe—the horn! We attack now!"

The first longbow arrow struck a searchlight and its glow grew dimmer as the arrow's burden—a thin tube of thick lance tree ink—splattered against it. Another followed——

Then the horn rang out, harsh and commanding, and in the distance a unicorn screamed in answer. The savage cry of a prowler came, like a sound to match, and the attack was on.

He ran with Fenrir beside him and to his left and right ran the others with their prowlers. The lead groups converged as they went through the wide gap in the wall. They ran on, into the dust cloud, and the shadowy forms of the Gerns were suddenly before them.

A blaster beam cut into them and a Gern shouted, "The natives!" Other beams sprang into life, winking like pale blue eyes through the dust and killing all they touched. The beams dropped as the first volley of arrows tore through the massed front ranks, to be replaced by others.

They charged on, into the blue winking of the blasters and the red lances of the flame guns with the crossbows rattling and strumming in answer. The prowlers lunged and fought beside them and ahead of them; black hell-creatures that struck the Gerns too swiftly for blasters to find before throats were torn out; the sound of battle turned into a confusion of raging snarls, frantic shouts and dying screams.

A prowler shot past him to join Fenrir—Sigyn—and he felt Tip dart up to his shoulder. She made a sound of greeting in passing, a sound that was gone as her jaws closed on a Gern.

The dust cloud cleared a little and the searchlights looked down on the scene; no longer brilliantly white but shining through the red-black lance tree ink as a blood red glow. A searchlight turret slid shut and opened a moment later, the light wiped clean. The longbows immediately transformed it into a red glow.

The beam of one of the turret blasters stabbed down, to blaze a trail of death through the battle. It ceased as its own light revealed to the Gern commander that the Ragnarok forces were so intermixed with the Gern forces that he was killing more Gerns than Ragnarok men.

By then the fighting was so hand to hand that knives were better than crossbows. The Gerns fell like harvested corn; too slow and awkward to use their bayonets against the faster Ragnarok men and killing as many of one another as men when they tried to use their blasters and flame guns. From the rear there came the command of a Gern officer, shouted high and thin above the sound of battle:

139

"Back to the ship—leave the natives for the ship's blasters to kill!"

The unicorns arrived then, to cut off their retreat.

They came twenty from the east and twenty from the west in a thunder of hooves, squealing and screaming in their blood lust, with prowlers a black wave going before them. They struck the Gerns; the prowlers slashing lanes through them while the unicorns charged behind, trampling them, ripping into them with their horns and smashing them down with their hooves as they vented the pent up rage of their years of confinement. On the back of each was a rider whose long spear flicked and stabbed into the throats and bellies of Gerns.

The retreat was halted and transformed into milling confusion. He led his own groups in the final charge, the prearranged wedge attack, and they split the Gern force in two.

The ship was suddenly just beyond them.

He gave the last command to Lake and Craig: "Now—into the ship!"

He scooped up a blaster from beside a fallen Gern and ran toward it. A Gern officer was already in the airlock, his face pale and strained as he looked back and his hand on the closing switch. He shot him and ran up the ramp as the officer's body rolled down it.

Unicorn hooves pounded behind him and twenty of them swept past, their riders leaping from their backs to the ramp. Twenty men and fifteen prowlers charged up the ramp as a warning siren shrieked somewhere inside the ship. At the same time the airlocks, operated from the control room, began to slide swiftly shut.

He was through first, with Fenrir and Sigyn. Lake and Craig, together with six men and four prowlers, squeezed through barely in time. Then the airlocks were closed and they were sealed in the ship.

Alarm bells added their sound to the shrieking of the siren and from the multiple-compartments shafts came the whir of elevators dropping with Gern forces to kill the humans trapped inside the ship.

They ran past the elevator shafts without pausing, light and swift in the artificial gravity that was only two-thirds that of Ragnarok. They

140

split forces as long ago planned; three men and four prowlers going with Charley Craig in the attempt to take the drive room, Lake and the other three men going with him in the attempt to take the control room.

They found the manway ladder and began to climb, Fenrir and Sigyn impatiently crowding their heels.

There was nothing on the control room level and they ran down the short corridor that their maps had showed. They turned left, into the corridor that had the control room at its end, and into the concentrated fire of nine waiting Gerns.

Fenrir and Sigyn went into the Gerns, under their fire before they could drop the muzzles of their blasters, with an attack so vicious and unexpected that what would have been a certain and lethal trap for the humans was suddenly a fighting chance.

The corridor became an inferno of blaster beams that cracked and hissed as they met and crossed, throwing little chips of metal from the walls with snapping sounds and going through flesh with sounds like soft tappings. It was over within seconds, the last Gern down and one man still standing beside him, the blond and nerveless Lake.

Thomsen and Barber were dead and Billy West was bracing himself against the wall with a blaster hole through his stomach, trying to say something and sliding to the floor before it was ever spoken.

And Sigyn was down, blood welling and bubbling from a wound in her chest, while Fenrir stood over her with his snarling a raging scream as he swung his head in search of a still-living Gern.

Humbolt and Lake ran on, Fenrir raging beside them, and into the control room.

Six officers, one wearing the uniform of a commander, were gaping in astonishment and bringing up their blasters in the way that seemed so curiously slow to Humbolt. Fenrir, in his fury, killed two of them as Lake's blaster and his own killed three more.

The commander was suddenly alone, his blaster half lifted. Fenrir leaped at his throat and Humbolt shouted the quick command: "Disarm!"

141

It was something the prowlers had been taught in their training and Fenrir's teeth clicked short of the commander's throat while his paw sent the blaster spinning across the room.

The commander stared at them with his swarthy face a dark gray and his mouth still gaping.

"How—how did you do it?" he asked in heavily accented Terran. "Only two of you——"

"Don't talk until you're asked a question," Lake said.

"Only two of you...." The thought seemed to restore his courage, as sight of the ship had restored Narth's that night, and his tone became threatening. "There are only two of you and more guards will be here to kill you within a minute. Surrender to me and I'll let you go free——"

Lake slapped him across the mouth with a backhanded blow that snapped his head back on his shoulders and split his lip.

"Don't talk," he ordered again. "And never lie to us."

The commander spit out a tooth and held his hand to his bleeding mouth. He did not speak again.

Tip and Freckles were holding tightly to his shoulder and each other, the racing of their hearts like a vibration, and he touched them reassuringly.

"All right now—all safe now," he said.

He called Charley Craig. "Charley—did you make it?"

"We made it to the drive room—two of us and one prowler," Charley answered. "What about you?"

"Norman and I have the control room. Cut their drives, to play safe. I'll let you know as soon as the entire ship is ours."

He went to the viewscreen and saw that the battle was over. Chiara was letting the searchlight burn again and prowlers were being used to drive back the unicorns from the surrendering Gerns.

142

"I guess we won," he said to Lake.

But there was no feeling of victory, none of the elation he had thought he would have. Sigyn was dying alone in the alien corridor outside. Sigyn, who had nursed beside him and fought beside him and laid down her life for him....

"I want to look at her," he said to Lake.

Fenrir went with him. She was still alive, waiting for them to come back to her. She lifted her head and touched his hand with her tongue as he examined the wound.

It was not fatal—it need not be fatal. He worked swiftly, gently, to stop the bleeding that had been draining her life away. She would have to lie quietly for weeks but she would recover.

When he was done he pressed her head back to the floor and said, "Lie still, Sigyn girl, until we can come to move you. Wait for us and Fenrir will stay here with you."

She obeyed and he left them, the feeling of victory and elation coming to him in full then.

Lake looked at him questioningly as he entered the control room and he said, "She'll live."

He turned to the Gern commander. "First, I want to know how the war is going?"

"I——" The commander looked uncertainly at Lake.

"Just tell the truth," Lake said. "Whether you think we'll like it or not."

"We have all the planets but Earth, itself," the commander said. "We'll have it, soon."

"And the Terrans on Athena?"

"They're still—working for us there."

"Now," he said, "you will order every Gern in this ship to go to his sleeping quarters. They will leave their weapons in the corridors

143

outside and they will not resist the men who will come to take charge of the ship."

The commander made an effort toward defiance:

"And if I refuse?"

Lake answered, smiling at him with the smile of his that was no more than a quick showing of teeth and with the savage eagerness in his eyes.

"If you refuse I'll start with your fingers and break every bone to your shoulders. If that isn't enough I'll start with your toes and go to your hips. And then I'll break your back."

The commander hesitated, sweat filming his face as he looked at them. Then he reached out to switch on the all-stations communicator and say into it:

"Attention, all personnel: You will return to your quarters at once, leaving your weapons in the corridors. You are ordered to make no resistance when the natives come...."

There was a silence when he had finished and Humbolt and Lake looked at each other, bearded and clad in animal skins but standing at last in the control room of a ship that was theirs: in a ship that could take them to Athena, to Earth, to the ends of the galaxy.

The commander watched them, on his face the blankness of unwillingness to believe.

"The airlocks—" he said. "We didn't close them in time. We never thought you would dare try to take the ship—not savages in animal skins."

"I know," Humbolt answered. "We were counting on you to think that way."

"No one expected any of you to survive here." The commander wiped at his swollen lips, wincing, and an almost child-like petulance came into his tone. "You weren't supposed to survive."

"I know," he said again. "We've made it a point to remember that."

144

"The gravity, the heat and cold and fever, the animals—why didn't they kill you?"

"They tried," he said. "But we fought back. And we had a goal—to meet you Gerns again. You left us on a world that had no resources. Only enemies who would kill us—the gravity, the prowlers, the unicorns. So we made them our resources. We adapted to the gravity that was supposed to kill us and became stronger and quicker than Gerns. We made allies of the prowlers and unicorns who were supposed to be our executioners and used them tonight to help us kill Gerns. So now we have your ship."

"Yes ... you have our ship." Through the unwillingness to believe on the commander's face and the petulance there came the triumph of vindictive anticipation. "The savages of Ragnarok have a Gern cruiser—but what can they do with it?"

"What can we do with it?" he asked, almost kindly. "We've planned for two hundred years what we can do with it. We have the cruiser and sixty days from now we'll have Athena. That will be only the beginning and you Gerns are going to help us do it."

For six days the ship was a scene of ceaseless activity. Men crowded it, asking questions of the Gern officers and crew and calmly breaking the bones of those who refused to answer or who gave answers that were not true. Prowlers stalked the corridors, their cold yellow eyes watching every move the Gerns made. The little mockers began roaming the ship at will, unable any longer to restrain their curiosity and confident that the men and prowlers would not let the Gerns harm them.

One mocker was killed then; the speckle-faced mocker that could repeat messages verbatim. It wandered into a storage cubicle where a Gern was working alone and gave him the opportunity to safely vent his hatred of everything associated with the men of Ragnarok. He broke its back with a steel bar and threw it, screaming, into the disposal chute that led to the matter converter. A prowler heard the scream and an instant later the Gern screamed; a sound that died in its making as the prowler tore his throat out. No more mockers were harmed.

One Ragnarok boy was killed. Three fanatical Gern officers stole knives from the galley and held the boy as hostage for their freedom. When their demands were refused they cut his heart out. Lake cornered them a few minutes later and, without touching his blaster, disemboweled them with their own knives. He smiled down upon them as they writhed and moaned on the floor and their moans were heard for a long time by the other Gerns in the ship before they died. No more humans were harmed.

They discovered that operation of the cruiser was relatively simple, basically similar to the operation of Terran ships as described in the text book the original Lake had written. Most of the operations were performed by robot mechanisms and the manual operations, geared to the slower reflexes of the Gerns, were easily mastered.

They could spend the forty-day voyage to Athena in further learning and practice so on the sixth day they prepared to depart. The unicorns had been given the freedom they had fought so well for and reconnaissance vehicles were loaned from the cruiser to take their place. Later there would be machinery and supplies of all kinds brought in by freighter ships from Athena.

Time was precious and there was a long, long job ahead of them. They blasted up from Ragnarok on the morning of the seventh day and went into the black sea of hyperspace.

By then the Gern commander was no longer of any value to them. His unwillingness to believe that savages had wrested his ship from him had increased until his compartment became his control room to him and he spent the hours laughing and giggling before an imaginary viewscreen whereon the cruiser's blasters were destroying, over and over, the Ragnarok town and all the humans in it.

But Narth, who had wanted to have them tortured to death for daring to resist capture, became very cooperative. In the control room his cooperation was especially eager. On the twentieth day of the voyage they let him have what he had been trying to gain by subterfuge: access to the transmitter when no men were within hearing distance.

After that his manner abruptly changed. Each day his hatred for them and his secret anticipation became more evident.

The thirty-fifth day came, with Athena five days ahead of them—the day of the execution they had let him arrange for them.

Stars filled the transdimensional viewscreen, the sun of Athena in the center. Humbolt watched the space to the lower left and the flicker came again; a tiny red dot that was gone again within a microsecond, so quickly that Narth in the seat beside him did not see it.

It was the quick peek of another ship; a ship that was running invisible with its detector screens up but which had had to drop them for an instant to look out at the cruiser. Not even the Gerns had ever been able to devise a polarized detector screen.

He changed the course and speed of the cruiser, creating an increase in gravity which seemed very slight to him but which caused Narth to slew heavily in his seat. Narth straightened and he said to him:

"Within a few minutes we'll engage the ship you sent for."

Narth's jaw dropped, then came back up. "So you spied on me?"

"One of our Ragnarok allies did—the little animal that was sitting near the transmitter. They're our means of communication. We learned that you had arranged for a ship, en route to Athena, to intercept us and capture us."

"So you know?" Narth asked. He smiled, an unpleasant twisting of his mouth. "Do you think that knowing will help you any?"

"We expect it to," he answered.

"It's a battleship," Narth said. "It's three times the size of this cruiser, the newest and most powerful battleship in the Gern fleet. How does that sound to you?"

"It sounds good," he said. "We'll make it our flagship."

"Your flagship—your 'flagship'!" The last trace of pretense left Narth and he let his full and rankling hatred come through. "You got this cruiser by trickery and learned how to operate it after a fashion because of an animal-like reflex abnormality. For forty-two days you accidental mutants have given orders to your superiors and thought you were our equals. Now, your fool's paradise is going to end."

The red dot came again, closer, and he once more altered the ship's

147

course. He had turned on the course analyzer and it clicked as the battleship's position was correlated with that of its previous appearance. A short yellow line appeared on the screen to forecast its course for the immediate future.

"And then?" he asked curiously, turning back to Narth.

"And then we'll take all of you left alive back to your village. The scenes of what we do to you and your village will be televised to all Gern-held worlds. It will be a valuable reminder for any who have forgotten the penalty for resisting Gerns."

The red dot came again. He punched the BATTLE STATIONS button and the board responded with a row of READY lights.

"All the other Gerns are by now in their acceleration couches," he said. "Strap yourself in for high acceleration maneuvers—we'll make contact with the battleship within two minutes."

Narth did so, taking his time as though it was something of little importance. "There will be no maneuvers. They'll blast the stern and destroy your drive immediately upon attack."

He fastened the last strap and smiled, taunting assurance in the twisted unpleasantness of it. "The appearance of this battleship has very much disrupted your plans to strut like conquering heroes among the slaves on Athena, hasn't it?"

"Not exactly," Humbolt replied. "Our plans are a little broader in scope than that. There are two new cruisers on Athena, ready to leave the shops ten days from now. We'll turn control of Athena over to the humans there, of course, then we'll take the three cruisers and the battleship back by way of Ragnarok. There we'll pick up all the Ragnarok men who are neither too old nor too young and go on to Earth. They will be given training en route in the handling of ships. We expect to find no difficulty in breaking through the Gern lines around Earth and then, with the addition of the Earth ships, we can easily capture all the Gern ships in the solar system."

"'Easily'!" Narth made a contemptuous sneer of the word. "Were you actually so stupid as to think that you biological freaks could equal Gern officers who have made a career of space warfare?"

"We'll far exceed them," he said. "A space battle is one of trying to keep your blaster beams long enough on one area of the enemy ship to break through its blaster shields at that point. And at the same time try to move and dodge fast enough to keep the enemy from doing the same thing to you. The ships are capable of accelerations up to fifty gravities or more but the acceleration limitator is the safeguard that prevents the ship from going into such a high degree of acceleration or into such a sudden change of direction that it would kill the crew.

"We from Ragnarok are accustomed to a one point five gravity and can withstand much higher degrees of acceleration than Gerns or any other race from a one gravity world. To enable us to take advantage of that fact we have had the acceleration limitator on this cruiser disconnected."

"Disconnected?" Narth's contemptuous regard vanished in frantic consternation. "You fool—you don't know what that means—you'll move the acceleration lever too far and kill us all!"

The red dot flicked on the viewscreen, trembled, and was suddenly a gigantic battleship in full view. He touched the acceleration control and Narth's next words were cut off as his diaphragm sagged. He swung the cruiser in a curve and Narth was slammed sideways, the straps cutting into him and the flesh of his face pulled lopsided by the gravity. His eyes, bulging, went blank with unconsciousness.

The powerful blasters of the battleship blossomed like a row of pale blue flowers, concentrating on the stern of the cruiser. A warning siren screeched as they started breaking through the cruiser's shields. He dropped the detector screen that would shield the cruiser from sight, but not from the blaster beams, and tightened the curve until the gravity dragged heavily at his own body.

The warning siren stopped as the blaster beams of the battleship went harmlessly into space, continuing to follow the probability course plotted from the cruiser's last visible position and course by the battleship's robot target tracers.

He lifted the detector screen, to find the battleship almost exactly where the cruiser's course analyzers had predicted it would be. The blasters of the battleship were blazing their full concentration of firepower into an area behind and to one side of the cruiser.

149

They blinked out at sight of the cruiser in its new position and blazed again a moment later, boring into the stern. He dropped the detector screen and swung the cruiser in another curve, spiraling in the opposite direction. As before, the screech of the alarm siren died as the battleship's blasters followed the course given them by course analyzers and target tracers that were built to presume that all enemy ships were acceleration-limitator equipped.

The cruiser could have destroyed the battleship at any time—but they wanted to capture their flagship unharmed. The maneuvering continued, the cruiser drawing closer to the battleship. The battleship, in desperation, began using the same hide-and-jump tactics the cruiser used but it was of little avail—the battleship moved at known acceleration limits and the cruiser's course analyzers predicted each new position with sufficient accuracy.

The cruiser made its final dash in a tightening spiral, its detector screen flickering on and off. It struck the battleship at a matched speed, with a thump and ringing of metal as the magnetic grapples fastened the cruiser like a leech to the battleship's side.

In that position neither the forward nor stern blasters of the battleship could touch it. There remained only to convince the commander of the battleship that further resistance was futile.

This he did with a simple ultimatum to the commander:

"This cruiser is firmly attached to your ship, its acceleration limitator disconnected. Its drives are of sufficient power to thrust both ships forward at a much higher degree of acceleration than persons from one-gravity worlds can endure. You will surrender at once or we shall be forced to put these two ships into a curve of such short radius and at an acceleration so great that all of you will be killed."

Then he added, "If you surrender we'll do somewhat better by you than you did with the humans two hundred years ago—we'll take all of you on to Athena."

The commander, already sick from an acceleration that would have been negligible to Ragnarok men, had no choice.

His reply came, choked with acceleration sickness and the greater sickness of defeat:

150

"We will surrender."

Narth regained consciousness. He saw Humbolt sitting beside him as before, with no Gern rescuers crowding into the control room with shouted commands and drawn blasters.

"Where are they?" he asked. "Where is the battleship?"

"We captured it," he said.

"You captured—a Gern battleship?"

"It wasn't hard," he said. "It would have been easier if only Ragnarok men had been on the cruiser. We didn't want to accelerate to any higher gravities than absolutely necessary because of the Gerns on it."

"You did it—you captured the battleship," Narth said, his tone like one dazed.

He wet his lips, staring, as he contemplated the unpleasant implications of it.

"You're freak mutants who can capture a battleship. Maybe you will take Athena and Earth from us. But"—the animation of hatred returned to his face—"What good will it do you? Did you ever think about that?"

"Yes," he said. "We've thought about it."

"Have you?" Narth leaned forward, his face shining with the malice of his gloating. "You can never escape the consequences of what you have done. The Gern Empire has the resources of dozens of worlds. The Empire will build a fleet of special ships, a force against which your own will be nothing, and send them to Earth and Athena and Ragnarok. The Empire will smash you for what you have done and if there are any survivors of your race left they will cringe before Gerns for a hundred generations to come.

"Remember that while you're posturing in your little hour of glory on Athena and Earth."

"You insist in thinking we'll do as Gerns would do," he said. "We

151

won't delay to do any posturing. We'll have a large fleet when we leave Earth and we'll go at once to engage the Gern home fleet. I thought you knew we were going to do that. We're going to cripple and capture your fleet and then we're going to destroy your empire."

"Destroy the Empire—now?" Narth stared again, all the gloating gone as he saw, at last, the quick and inexorable end. "Now—before we can stop you—before we can have a chance?"

"When a race has been condemned to die by another race and it fights and struggles and manages somehow to survive, it learns a lesson. It learns it must never again let the other race be in position to destroy it. So this is the harvest you reap from the seeds you sowed on Ragnarok two hundred years ago.

"You understand, don't you?" he asked, almost gently. "For two hundred years the Gern Empire has been a menace to our survival as a race. Now, the time has come when we shall remove it."

He stood in the control room of the battleship and watched Athena's sun in the viewscreen, blazing like a white flame. Sigyn, fully recovered, was stretched out on the floor near him; twitching and snarling a little in her sleep as she fought again the battle with the Gerns. Fenrir was pacing the floor, swinging his black, massive head restlessly, while Tip and Freckles were examining with fascinated curiosity the collection of bright medals that had been cleaned out of the Gern commander's desk.

Lake and Craig left their stations, as impatient as Fenrir, and came over to watch the viewscreen with him.

"One day more," Craig said. "We're two hundred years late but we're coming in to the world that was to have been our home."

"It can never be, now," he said. "Have any of us ever thought of that—that we're different to humans and there's no human world we could ever call home?"

"I've thought of it," Lake said. "Ragnarok made us different physically and different in the way we think. We could live on human worlds—but we would always be a race apart and never really belong there."

152

"I suppose we've all thought about it," Craig said. "And wondered what we'll do when we're finished with the Gerns. Not settle down on Athena or Earth, in a little cottage with a fenced-in lawn where it would be adventure to watch the Three-D shows after each day at some safe, routine job."

"Not back to Ragnarok," Lake said. "With metals and supplies from other worlds they'll be able to do a lot there but the battle is already won. There will be left only the peaceful development—building a town at the equator for Big Winter, leveling land, planting crops. We could never be satisfied with that kind of a life."

"No," he said, and felt his own restlessness stir in protest at the thought of settling down in some safe and secure environment. "Not Athena or Earth or Ragnarok—not any world we know."

"How long until we're finished with the Gerns?" Lake asked. "Ten years? We'll still be young then. Where will we go—all of us who fought the Gerns and all of the ones in the future who won't want to live out their lives on Ragnarok? Where is there a place for us—a world of our own?"

"Where do we find a world of our own?" he asked, and watched the star clouds creep toward them in the viewscreen; tumbled and blazing and immense beyond conception.

"There's a galaxy for us to explore," he said. "There are millions of suns and thousands of worlds waiting for us. Maybe there are races out there like the Gerns—and maybe there are races such as we were a hundred years ago who need our help. And maybe there are worlds out there with things on them such as no man ever imagined.

"We'll go, to see what's there. Our women will go with us and there will be some worlds on which some of us will want to stay. And, always, there will be more restless ones coming from Ragnarok. Out there are the worlds and the homes for all of us."

"Of course," Lake said. "Beyond the space frontier ... where else would we ever belong?"

It was all settled, then, and there was a silence as the battleship plunged through hyperspace, the cruiser running beside her and

153

their drives moaning and thundering as had the drives of the Constellation two hundred years before.

A voyage had been interrupted then, and a new race had been born. Now they were going on again, to Athena, to Earth, to the farthest reaches of the Gern Empire. And on, to the wild, unknown regions of space beyond.

There awaited their worlds and there awaited their destiny; to be a race scattered across a hundred thousand light-years of suns, to be an empire such as the galaxy had never known.

They, the restless ones, the unwanted and forgotten, the survivors.

THE END

CPSIA information can be obtained
at www.ICGtesting.com
Printed in the USA
BVHW040001050123
655621BV00011B/43/J

9 781644 399743